TIME AND TIME AGAIN
A Time Traveller's Tales

*A Science Fiction, Action Adventure Novella
by Michael John Siddall.
Copyright © 28th March 2013*

Text copyright © Michael J Siddall 2014

Cover Art copyright © Alexander Lawson 2014

Proofreaders: Olivia Siddall & Ben Siddall-Ward

All rights reserved

The moral right of the author and illustrator have been asserted

Condition of sale

This book is sold subject to the condition that it shall not, by way of trade or otherwise, be lent, resold, hired out or otherwise circulated without the author's prior written consent in any form of binding or cover other than that in which it is published and without a similar condition including this condition being imposed on the subsequent purchaser.

For BEN and OLIVIA.

LOOSE ENDS...

"Hello! My name is Ben Ward and I am a real Time Traveller who tinkered together a Time Machine in my later years, due to technological advances in the field of physics and my hard work at Cal.Tech.

"I eventually sent the Machine back to my younger-self in the hope of saving my wife from a maniac called Frankie Boyle. He murdered her. She was a Psychological Profiler and undercover police officer with Special Branch, who had gone deep undercover to further her career in the hope of catching Frankie – a psychopathic serial killer.

"She was brutally murdered in the process of her duties, but I did what no other person on earth could do! I caught Frankie myself and dumped his ass in the far flung future, before he could murder Jane, and I left him there to die a coward's death, thus reversing time, regaining my idyllic life by getting my beautiful wife back.

"You see, Jane's always been devoted to me, and I to her and the children, but when she went undercover I didn't know, because she wasn't allowed to leak any information, even to me, under any circumstances. But that's how Special Branch works, I guess.

"Now life is fun again! A game! An adventure! Particularly if you happen to be a Time Traveller, like me, with all the time in the world and can do the most enjoyable things – time and time again!

"You see, I had at first thought time travel impossible, like most rational beings, but then discovered it is possible with the aid of a machine no bigger than a calculator, made of brass, nickel and ivory.

"Now the machine and I go skipping through the centuries, even though initially I had to be calm and not travel too far or too fast in case the machine had limitations that might cause me great harm, or worse – kill me!

"And so, I propel myself through the Fourth Dimension with the speed of a bullet whenever I can, like a vapour through thin air, ghostlike and unnoticed, and my greatest worry is of coming to a jarring halt inside something solid, smashing me to pieces. However, the compelling feeling of time travel is of being born, over and over again – traumatic, yet amazing!

"Leaping from one century to the next in the blink of an eye, I have conversed at length with Doctor Who when he was a mere boy, helped H.G.Wells write 'The Time Machine' when he was a struggling author and spent valuable moments solving the riddles of an age – and my only fear is of the Unknown! But I can and do control that fear, simply because I must!"

Chapter 1

It's Sunday and early afternoon. The date is the 18th of June. And the year is 1815. I'm near Waterloo in Belgium, part of the United Kingdom of the Netherlands, and I'm watching the Imperial French Army, under the command of Emperor Napoleon, being defeated by the armies of the Seventh Coalition, comprising of an Anglo-Allied force under the command of the Duke of Wellington, combined with a Prussian army under the command of Gebhard von Blucher.

This battle I'm watching will be Napoleon's last campaign and his defeat at Waterloo will conclude his rule as Emperor of the French, marking the end of his *One Hundred Day* return from exile.

Two huge forces under Wellington and Blucher have assembled close to the north-eastern border of France, while Napoleon chooses to attack first in the hope of destroying them before they can join with the other members of the coalition in a coordinated invasion of France.

This decisive engagement at Waterloo began on the 16th and will end on the 19th of this month of June, and according to Wellington will be – and I quote: "the nearest run thing you will ever see in your life." At least, that's what he told me.

Napoleon has delayed giving battle until now to allow the muddy ground time to dry, while Wellington's army is positioned across the Brussels road on the Mont-Saint-Jeane escarpment, withstanding and repelling small repeated attacks from the French.

"This evening the Prussians will arrive in force and break through Napoleon's right flank," I tell Wellington with an air of impartiality. "And at that moment, your Anglo-Allied army must attack and drive the French army in disorder from the field of battle!"

He stares at me with a look of suspicion. "Are you a fortune teller, sir?"

I shake my head stiffly. "No! I'm a *Time Traveller*, armed with the knowledge of what you must do to win this campaign. And if you do what I say, pursuing Coalition forces will enter France and restore King Louis to the French throne. Napoleon will then abdicate and surrender to the British. Later he will be exiled to Saint Helena, where he will die in 1821."

The Duke stares at me again like I'm a half-wit. "A Time Traveller, sir? Do you really expect me to believe such nonsense. Admittedly you dress rather oddly and appeared among the British ranks under strange circumstances, but do you really expect me to believe you're from the future and know what is about to take place here?"

My dark eyes must be shining and twinkling and my pale face must be flushed and animated, I think to myself. "But it's the truth, my dear Duke!" I tell him.

He begins slapping his thighs, laughing with great gusto. "Well, I'll be a monkey's uncle. I've heard everything now!" he says. "Is it not rather a large thing to expect me to believe that your real existence is in the future, sir?"

"I arrived here this morning, quite by accident, when my Time Machine had a hissy-fit and propelled me through the Fourth Dimension to the *wrong* time and place, nothing more and nothing less," I say. "However, to prove what I'm telling you is true I tell you this, as a part-time historian I know that your initial disposition this morning was to counter Napoleon's threat of enveloping the Coalition armies by moving them to Mons, south-west of Brussels. This in effect would cut your communications with your base at Ostend, but would also push your army closer to Blucher's. I also know that Napoleon manipulated your fear of the loss of your supply chain from the channel ports with false information from embedded spies. Need I go on? Or do you now believe I *am* a fortune teller and not a Time Traveller?"

Wellington scratches his head. "That's exactly what I *was* thinking when I woke up this morning, and I told no one! Goddamnit! How the hell could you know what I was thinking?"

I smile to myself faintly. "Now do you believe my story?"

He nods his head, eyes wide. "What will Napoleon and his forces do today?" he asks in a whisper.

I stare him squarely in the eyes. "He will *lose,* because of the admirable resolve of the British army and Coalition forces; because of the bad weather conditions and muddy ground, and because he doesn't attack in the morning and strike while the iron is hot," I tell Wellington as I put my hand into my deep coat pocket, producing my machine with its parts of brass, nickel and ivory, its size no larger than a calculator.

Wellington watches me reset it. I press the relevant buttons and drift off like a ghost. My heart is beating fast, it's hard to catch my breath and the last thing I see before everything goes black and I pass out is Wellington's disbelieving gaze, staring at me as I vanish right before his eyes. I wasn't born until 1962, exactly 147 years after the Battle of Waterloo, so my tale is a strange one to tell. However, it's one that's worth listening to, if you have the time. Well do you? Because I have all the time in the world to tell it!

Chapter 2

Please let me introduce myself. My name is Ben Ward, and I *am* a Time Traveller. The year is 2012 A.D. and I'm fifty years old, tall and muscular with dark eyes, greying hair and I'm good looking but not handsome. I'm a quiet, scholarly man, broad-shouldered, strong, well-coordinated and quick when I need to be. And my adventures began two years ago to the day when I received a catalogue called Time Unlimited. It was a day that changed my life forever – and a day I would never forget.

Up until that day my greatest achievement had been taking the Bar Exam to become a barrister-at-law (a lawyer), and my worst living nightmare had been the murder of my wife Jane at the hands of a crazed killer. But when I bought an odd, one of a kind Sat-Nav, made of brass, nickel and ivory from a mysterious online company called TimeLine, something very bizarre happened – the machine talked to me, announcing that it was a Time Machine. And it was!

I quickly learned how to manipulate the Time Machine and *Time* in the past, present and future and managed to stop my wife's murder, but then I discovered that I wasn't the only Time Traveller. I had, in my old age, built a Sub-Atomic Time-Navigator. A Time Travelling Crash Dummy, if you like.

Yes, I had not only devised the Time Machine with all of its intricate parts, but *I* had also tinkered together the most complicated and awesome piece of machinery ever devised by humans. Nav-Man. A robot of somewhat large proportions. And so, my adventures continue as I travel the eons in search of answers to more unanswered questions, and the riddles of an age, even though the peculiar sensation of time-travelling is excessively unpleasant.

It's a feeling like no other: one of a helpless, headlong, motion with an imminent crash coming. One of weightlessness and flying, like riding a huge switchback that's trying to pull free of a Black Hole. It makes your eyes bulge, lungs burn and it's hard to breathe.

The effect as I go forward or backward in time is of night following day, like the flapping of a butterfly's wing, but the dim shadows of my surroundings in the *present day* are always looming somewhere in the background for me to hear, see and smell, but not touch or taste when I'm time-travelling in my Spectral Form. And as the machine puts on pace, I see the sun hopping across the sky, marking a whole day in much less than a minute, then the twinkling succession of the moon spinning through its phases from new to full, with faint glimpses of the circling constellations gaining great velocity as they travel through the night sky.

Tall buildings rise and fall before my eyes in landscapes that are misty and vague. Hills become valleys, mountains become seas; grasslands become deserts and all in the blink of an eye.

I watch trees growing old in seconds as they spread, wither and pass away, and the whole surface of the earth seems to change, melting and flowing away right before me. Then, I'm travelling far too fast to be conscious of any living or moving thing. Finally everything grows faint, ghostlike and as I draw a breath and grit my teeth the buzzing from the machine grows louder and the vibrating stops. I'm off at the speed of thought through the vast wormholes of *time* and complete darkness engulfs everything. I usually pass out at this point, because of the awful, nauseous, sickly feeling that overcomes me – and I'm glad when I do!

After a brief moment, I come back to my senses; my mind reels in a kind of fog and once again I feel the weight of my body as in a falling sensation. There is usually a flash of blinding light too and a great confusion of noise around me as I open my eyes. Then I'm there, wherever I want to be.

Well, now I spend my days leaping from century to century, fine tuning my time-travelling skills even more, and I've found that I can disappear from one time era and go anywhere in the blink of an eye, because with the Sat-Nav in my hands I'm armed with a power beyond all possible reason. And that reminds me *where* I want to go next. A good friend of mine committed suicide twenty-five years ago, so I'm going back to the hour before he gave up God's greatest gift – his life.

Putting my hand into my deep coat pocket I produce my Time Machine, turning it on, and it buzzes loudly and vibrates in my hand. The familiar voice asks, "Space Time Coordinates?" However, I have no idea what the Space Time Coordinates are, so I relay to the machine the information I have written down.

"*Calculating,*" it says flatly in its metallic sounding voice.

"Great," say I, smiling like a Cheshire Cat.

Suddenly, there seems to be a breath of wind in my flat, but there are no windows open and even though the lights aren't switched on they flicker once or twice. The room becomes indistinct and my reflection in the mirror is hazy, flickering in and out of sight. Then everything is silent for a moment as my form vanishes completely from the mirror. And off I go, propelling myself through the Fourth Dimension with the speed of a bullet, passing out once again. Blackness engulfs me...

***

When I come to my senses it's snowing heavily. I stare at the sign in front of me, covered in icicles, welcoming me to Redwood Road, London. The year is 1987. Bells are ringing, *jingalingalinging,* and most of the town's residents are singing as I walk down the tree lined streets decorated with shining fairy lights and glowing lanterns. But then, it *is* Christmas Eve, after all.

I walk on past an old emporium, a bank and the crowded shops, finally reaching the brightly lit homes, and as the singing fades into the background I hear voices praying inside the houses.

"Rory O'Shea's one of the few good guys, but he needs help and guidance," I hear a man's voice say at the first house.

"Father, please help Rory," I hear another man's voice say at the next.

"Mother of God, help my good friend Rory O'Shea," comes a third.

I hear a woman's voice praying too. "Holy Spirit, if you *can* hear me, please help my son, Rory, tonight!"

Another man speaks quietly in a doorway, unaware of my presence. "Rory always helps others, and that's probably why he's in trouble tonight!"

I walk on, listening intently.

"Rory's a good man, he just needs a break!" another voice says.

I even hear his wife praying and sobbing somewhere in the distance. "I do love Rory, dear Father, I just can't live with him anymore, so watch over him tonight, wherever he is!"

In fact, there are so many people praying for Rory's soul and well-being that I feel positively dizzy and can't hear anything else. But then, that's all I'm supposed to hear, because the Time Machine magnifies the sounds to make it so.

An awful lot of people are praying for my friend on this most crucial of nights, but they don't know he's thinking of throwing away his life. And I only have an hour to change his mind.

He's strong-willed, quick-witted and doesn't suffer fools

gladly, even though he has the I.Q. of a rabbit and the simple faith of a child, so I wonder what he'll make of me when I try to talk him out of committing suicide. And that's an interesting thought, because I can't exactly approach him and say, "Hi, Rory, remember me, Ben Ward! Good luck in whatever you decide to do with your life for the next hour before you commit the ultimate sin!" Or, "Hi again, Rory, have you thought of making out a *Will* before doing yourself in!"

Not a good idea. I'm supposed to be here to help my friend and I don't think that would. By all accounts, Rory has been trying hard to do what's best for everyone and has come to grief. He was always a very selfless person and still is by the sound of it.

I stop at a local store, peering in through the window at Mr. Fowler, Rory's boss in this time era, who stares right through me and carries on doing his allotted chores. But then, being in my Spectral Form does have its advantages, because people can only see me if I want them to. Recently I found out that I can even make people sneeze and they don't know why, which is pretty funny. I can put thoughts in their heads too by whispering softly in their ears. But the one thing I can't do is change man's *Free Will,* ever. If I could, things would be so much simpler because now it's my turn to help a friend in need.

The problem I face is not that he's sick. No, it's actually much worse than that. He's discouraged because his wife's left him. And at precisely 11:45pm tonight, Rory will be seriously considering taking his own life, which means that I have just one hour to get re-acquainted with him, so I must hurry if I'm to accomplish my mission and save him.

I ask the Time Machine to give me a quick re-run of his history from when we were kids together, to get me up to speed and show me what has brought him to this point in his life. And as the mists of *time* and *space* clear before me in what looks like an amazing laser-light-show, I can see several children playing on a frozen lake with home-made sledges.

"Who are they?" I ask the machine.

"That's Rory and his brother playing with you and some of your old school pals, all aged twelve years old in 1974, and something important happens here that you *will* remember, so watch and listen carefully!"

"I am watching and listening and we were a bloody noisy bunch back then by the sound of it," say I.

"Yay! Yippee! Okay, boys, let's ride!" the pals shout.

"Who's the tall boy?" I ask.

"That's Rory, your problem, so *watch and listen!*" says the machine bluntly.

"Here comes the Bullet-Train, my brother," shouts Rory.

I stare at Michael, a sickly-looking pale boy with sandy hair and green eyes.

"I'm the Easy-Rider!" Michael shouts back, sitting on a sledge. He slides down the hill towards the frozen lake.

"Come on down!" shouts my younger-self. "Go boy, go!"

I watch Michael scoot down the hill like a rocket, out of control, onto the frozen lake and the next thing I know he's screaming and shouting as he breaks through the ice and tumbles into the freezing water.

"Help! Help! Help me Rory!" he shouts.

Rory stands for a moment, stunned, his heart pounding. Then he races out over the ice towards Michael as fast as he can, slipping and sliding as he goes. "Don't worry I'm coming," he shouts.

"Help! Help!" Michael calls.

"Hang on, I'm coming as quick as I can!" shouts Rory with our pals following. He jumps into the water without a second thought or a moment's hesitation while the pals make a human chain, stretching all the way back to the bank-side.

My Time Machine's gears and mechanisms click away as if in real thought. "Rory saves his brother's life, but it costs him his hearing in his left ear when he catches a cold and it gets infected, so it is weeks before he returns to his after-school job at the local store on the Old Kent Road," it says. "However, on his return and his first day back, he helps Mr. Fowler serve a steady stream of customers. Then, while he is staring out of the mullioned window into the street he notices a regal looking car rolling by. A Rolls Royce."

"Who's that?" asks Emma, a raven-haired school friend and customer. "Is it someone famous?"

Rory stops whistling. "No, that's Wilson Peabody's car, the richest and meanest skinflint in the whole of London!"

Emma stares at the gleaming gold car and sees an old man waving. She whistles. "Wow, he looks like a *king!*"

Suddenly, a strawberry blonde girl with shining blue eyes comes running into the store, taking a seat by the counter.

"Hello Rory, hello Emma," she says enthusiastically.

"Hello Julia," says Emma.

"Your usual bag of toffee?" asks Rory.

"Please," says Julia.

There's none on the shelf behind him, so he goes to fetch the toffee from a store-room at the back of the shop.

"I really like him," says Julia, studying his confident walk.

Emma shakes her head in dismay. "Is there a boy you don't like?"

Julia spins around on her stool and stares at Emma. "Actually I do like them all, but what's wrong with that?" she asks.

Rory reappears from the store-room and gives Julia the

toffee. She smiles at him through admiring eyes, handing him the exact money. "Help me down Rory?" she says, fluttering her eyelashes at him.

"Help you down?" he snaps with a pinched expression on his face. He storms off to the other side of the counter, punches the till register with his index finger and as the bell rings and the drawer shoots open he throws in the money. "Don't think so!"

By the time he turns around she's jumped down from her stool, run from the store and is gone. He breathes a sigh of relief.

"Made your mind up yet, Emma?" he asks in a small voice.

She smiles. "I'll take the chocolate ice-cream please, Rory."

"With coconut on top and a flake?" he asks.

She pulls a sour face. "Don't like coconut."

"You don't like coconut?" he says, his face a picture of disbelief. "Say, brain-dead, don't you know they come from Tahiti, near the Fiji islands in the Coral sea?"

She shakes her head as he bobs beneath the counter to pick up a travel magazine. She leans over the counter and whispers in his bad ear. "I know you can't hear me, Rory, but I'll love you forever and until the day I die."

He doesn't hear a thing. He just bobs back up, whistling merrily, placing the magazine on the counter top in front of her. "I'm going exploring someday, you watch," he says, his eyes fever bright. "You can come too, if you like."

She shrugs. "Oh, I don't know about that Rory," she says, wanting him to persuade her a little more.

He shrugs. "Well, suit yourself," he says flatly.

Suddenly, Mr. Fowler's gruff voice comes from a back room, startling them both.

"Rory O' Shea, stop that jibber-jabber and get in here now! You ain't doin' no explorin' today, you've an errand to run for me!"

"Yes, sir, right away," replies Rory respectfully and he carries on whistling.

"Get in here *right now* and stop that damn whistling. You're not being paid to be an entertainer!" Mr. Fowler's voice is slurred and agitated.

Rory runs to the back room. "No, sir, sorry," he says, staring at his boss who is obviously drunk and sobbing fitfully. He notices a newly delivered letter on the table in front of him. He reads it quickly without Mr. Fowler seeing him. It's addressed to: *Emil Fowler of Redwood Road and reads:*

> *We regret to inform you that your wife,*
> *Paula, died very suddenly today,*
> *killed in a hit-and-run car accident.*
> *Everything possible was done to save her,*
> *but we couldn't.*
> *We await your instructions.*
> *Edward Melville of Collingborn Hospital.*

Rory's eyes widen to encompass the word '*died*' and his eyes mist over. "Mr. Fowler, what can I do for you?" he asks sympathetically.

Mr. Fowler is filling a prescription ready for delivery. "Just wait a Goddamn minute!" he snaps in a temper.

"Anything I can do for you back here?" asks Rory looking sad.

Mr. Fowler stops what he's doing and glares at him through teary eyes. "No! Just wait will you?!" he snaps again, dropping the prescription onto the floor.

Rory kneels down to pick up the box of capsules Mr. Fowler has been filling with a blue powder. "I'll get them for you, sir," he offers.

Mr. Fowler carries on crying and sniffling, his eyes dark,

bleak and haunted. "Take those capsules over to the Ramsey household immediately, they're waiting for them," he orders, his voice slurring.

"Yes, sir, right away," says Rory.

Mr. Fowler slumps to a chair like a sack of cabbages, head in hands, crying even more fitfully. Rory turns around, noticing the label on the jar his boss has filled the capsules from. It's almost illegible, but his young eyes manage to read it. *Rat Poison* it says. He touches the rim of the jar with his forefinger, putting it to his own lips. It's bitter. And he's sure that it *is* rat poison and not the drug to treat the Flu.

"They have the Flu at the Ramsey house, don't they sir?" asks Rory, respectfully.

"Ye... yeah," Mr. Fowler stammers.

"Is it a *charge* or *cash?*" asks Rory, stalling for time, trying to think what to do.

Mr. Fowler looks at him through drunken, bleary, doll-like eyes. "It's a charge," he says again, staring at a recent photograph of his dead wife.

Rory plucks up his courage. "Sir, I think you've made a big mistake!"

"Oh, get on your way will you, boy!" yells Mr. Fowler, his temper rising.

"Yes, sir," says Rory, not knowing what else to say or do. He plucks his baseball cap from the coat-rack; staring back at his boss slumped in the chair, and he notices an advertisement on the wall behind Mr. Fowler, which reads: "Your dad knows best." And that told him exactly what he needed to do.

Chapter 3

Rory picks up the box of deadly capsules and runs out into the busy street, heading across to the O'Shea Brother's Loan Association, where he climbs the steps to the second floor and flings open the office door. His uncle Thomas stops him there with an outstretched arm. "Avast there Columbus, what course are ye on?" he says abruptly.

Rory looks startled. "I've got to see dad!"

Thomas bars his way. "Some other time!"

"It's very important!"

"There's a tempest going on in his office," says Thomas, "and it's turning into a raging storm..."

Suddenly, Tilly, a tall, auburn haired receptionist calls out, "Thomas, telephone!"

Thomas turns to face her. "Who is it?"

"Bank Examiner!" comes the reply.

Uncle Thomas's face hardens and turns pale. "Bank Examiner? Shite! I should have called him this morning, but I forgot. Switch it inside." He lets go of Rory and dashes off into his office.

Rory takes his chance and slips into his father's dusty old office. "I'm not asking for much, Mr. Peabody," he hears him say.

"No, you're practically begging and that's a whole lot worse if you ask me," says Mr. Peabody, a fat, flatulent, bald man with a hard stare, well into his seventies. He's sat in a rickety old wheelchair, his legs covered by a blanket, and his silver haired aid is stood by his side with his arms folded across his chest.

"All I'm asking for is a short extension on the loan," says Peter O'Shea, a tall, honest looking man with greying hair, blue eyes and elegant movements.

"Dad!" says Rory.

"Just a minute, son," replies Peter.

"Time's up!" says Mr. Peabody, smiling crookedly.

"Just one more month, that's all we need. I'll get the ten thousand pounds somehow," says Peter.

"Dad!"

"Just a minute."

"Have you put any real pressure on your account holders to pay their mortgages?" asks Mr. Peabody, wheeling his chair closer to Peter's desk.

"Times are hard, money's scarce and lots of people are out of work."

"Well then, foreclose on the ones unable to pay!" snaps Mr. Peabody.

"I won't do that. These families have children and it's Christmas Eve for God's sake!" says Peter looking saddened.

"Dad!" says Rory impatiently.

"Wait just one minute, son!" snaps his father.

Mr Peabody smiles crookedly for a second time. "They're not my children or my responsibility."

"But they are someone's children. And they deserve better," says Peter.

Mr. Peabody slams his fist down hard onto Peter's desk. "Are you running a business or a charity?" he snaps. "Because if it's a charity, you're not doing it with *my* money!"

Peter looks exasperated. "Mr. Peabody, why are you so hard hearted? You have no family or children and can't possibly spend all of the fortune you've already got."

"Oh, I suppose I should donate it to all the incompetent failures and losers like you and that drunken brother of yours, so you can spend it for me! What's his name? Thomas?" shouts Mr. Peabody in a high pitched voice.

"Dad's not a *failure* and Uncle Thomas' not a *drunkard*,

so you can't say that about either of them!" shouts Rory.

"Quiet," chastises his father.

"But, you're not a failure. You're the best and kindest man in the city," announces Rory.

"Run along, run along," says his father.

"You're better than Mr. Peabody," says Rory, "so, don't let him say that about you, dad."

"All right, son. All right. Thanks, I'll talk to you tonight," says Peter, ushering Rory out of the office, and he shuts the door in his face.

Rory is confused and doesn't know what to do, so he heads back to the store to confront Mr. Fowler with the poison capsules. When he gets there, his boss is already on the telephone being told that Rory hasn't arrived at the Ramsey household with the medicine.

"What? Why the medicine should have arrived by now," says a distraught Mr. Fowler. "I'll be over in five minutes with a fresh prescription."

Rory tugs at his employer's arm. "I didn't deliver the prescription. I *couldn't*."

Mr. Fowler glares at him angrily. "What game are you playing, you lazy brat? What have you done with those capsules?"

"I... You..." Rory stammers. A wave of nausea sweeps through him. He's breathing heavily, his heart thumping. Sweat trickles down the middle of his back and his armpits are damp and sting savagely.

"Didn't you hear me? Where are those capsules?" snaps Mr. Fowler, grabbing a bunch of Rory's shirt in his fist, pulling him eye to eye. He begins slapping him about the ear.

Emma is still in the store, watching Rory getting beat up. She has tears in her eyes. Unable to help Rory, she runs from the store sobbing.

"Why didn't you deliver them right away? Their boy's very sick!" shouts Mr. Fowler.

"You're hurting my sore ear," sobs Rory, trying to defend himself.

"You lazy good-for-nothing," says Mr. Fowler.

Rory manages to pull away from his employer. "Mr. Fowler, you don't know what you're doing. You put *rat poison* in those capsules. I know you're hurting because you got the letter about your wife's death and you're upset, but you *did* put something bad in those capsules. It wasn't your fault, but just take a look and see what you've done.'

Mr. Fowler snatches the box of capsules out of Rory's hand, takes one out and breaks it open. He puts it to his lips, tasting it. It's bitter. He recognises it as rat poison and falls back in shock, sniffling and sobbing, realising the implications of his actions. "Oh, my God! Oh, no, no! Oh Rory, Rory, I'm so sorry!" he says, putting his arms around the boy, cuddling him.

"Oh, Mr. Fowler, I won't ever tell anyone what you did," says Rory. "I know how bad you're feeling. I won't ever tell a soul, I promise. Hope to die!"

"Oh, Rory, Rory," sobs Mr. Fowler...

***

My Time Machine pauses the proceedings. I stare at it and shake my head. "What did you stop for?"

"Because we need to come forward in time now, to when Rory has grown into an adult," enlightens my machine.

The mists of *time* and *space* darken and deepen for a moment and when they clear, Rory, aged twenty-five, is in a London department store checking out suitcases. His friend, Joe, the storekeeper is showing him hand luggage.

"This is an overnight case, made from genuine cowhide, and it's got a sturdy lock," says Joe.

Rory shakes his head. "Nope, nope, nope! I need a *big* case. Now look Joe, I want one this big!" He stretches out his arms to the fullest extent.

My Time machine pauses the proceedings again. "Take a look at that man's face and note his wholesome good looks. That's your friend, Rory O'Shea! Recognise him?"

"Yeah, that's him," I say.

"It's a good face. A strong face. And he never let on about the poison capsules to anyone," says the machine.

"Not a single word. Not even to his closest pals, including me. But, did he ever explore exotic shores or marry Emma?" I ask.

"Well, you'll just have to wait and see," offered the machine, setting time in motion again.

***

"...A big case! I want a case big enough to pack a month's clothes in with plenty of room on the outside to stick fancy labels on from Turkey, Egypt, Italy, Greece and a whole lot of other places!" says Rory excitedly.

Joe nods. "I see, you want something as big as a flying carpet, huh?"

"Yeah, that's right," says Rory.

"Don't suppose you'd like this old second-hand case would you?" asks Joe, slamming a big, dusty, brown case down onto the counter top.

"Now you're talking. Hell, I could use that as a raft instead of catching an ocean liner," laughs Rory. "It only needs a sail on top! How much is it?"

"Not a single penny," says Joe smiling.

Rory cocks his head thoughtfully. "That's my bad ear, Joe. I could have sworn you said – *not a single penny!*"

Joe points to Rory's name engraved on the case. "That's right. That's what I said."

"Well, how come my name's already on the case?"

"It's a present from old man Fowler. Came down and picked it out himself."

Rory smiles. "Did he now? Well, what do you know about that? Isn't that just the kindest thing that anyone could do?"

"What ship are you booked on?" asks Joe.

"I'm shipping out on the old Kensington."

Joe chuckles. "You'll be lucky to get out of the harbor on that, never mind abroad to Europe!"

Rory smiles. "Okay, so I like old ships and have a passion for history, besides exotic places." He picks up the case and marches out of the store without a backward glance, heading in the direction of Mr. Fowler's store. Mere moments later, he arrives. The store is full of people, chatting and milling around, but he dashes straight over to his old boss and takes him by the hand, shaking it. "Hello Mr. Fowler, how're you?" he inquires. "Thanks ever-so-much for the suitcase, it's just what I was looking for."

"Don't mention it," says Mr. Fowler nodding.

"But it's so nice of you to think of me."

"Well, I hope you have a fantastic time travelling and seeing the world."

"Yeah, I will. I only wish I had a million pounds to take with me," says Rory with a warm smile. "Going to try and work my way around the world on tramp-steamers and merchant ships." He shakes Mr. Fowler's hand again and marches off, out of the store with a grin on his face, and as he walks down the main street his uncle Thomas in an upstairs window of the O'Shea loan building shouts, "Avast there Columbus, have you earned your sea legs yet?"

Tilly shouts from the same window, "Parlez-vous francais, mister O'Shea?"

Then his father pops his head out. "Send me some of those

saucy postcards from exotic places, will you?"

Rory holds up the suitcase and waves. Then he notices Tommy the taxi driver talking to Paul the policeman on the street corner. "Hey Tommy, I'm an important tourist today, how about driving me home in style?"

"No problemo! Hoppeth in, your *Holyiness!*" offers Tommy.

Paul opens the cab door. "There you are, your Highness."

"Thank you your *Lowliness,* right away," replies Rory climbing aboard.

Tommy smiles and turns the meter off. "I'll even put my *King of the Nobodies* hat on just for you, so that you feel even more special..."

Just then, a pretty young woman passes by. 'Hello Rory, it's a beautiful afternoon isn't it?' she remarks cheerfully.

"Well, hello Julia!" says Rory. "Hey, you look great in that pink dress!"

Julia stops and smiles. "What, this old thing? Why, I only wear this when I don't care how I look!" she says, flicking back her golden hair.

Tommy and Paul wolf-whistle as she walks off around the corner and disappears. All three men stare with their mouths hanging open.

"How would you like to...?" says Tommy.

"Yes, I would!" says Rory reading his thoughts. "I definitely would!"

"Want to come with us, Paul? I'll show you both the sights," says Tommy.

Paul shakes his head and wolf-whistles again. "No, I've seen enough sights for one day. I'm going home to my wife, and I'm going to close my eyes and imagine she's Julia."

All three men laugh.

"Tommy shakes his head. *"Wise-guy!"*

***

SOMEWHERE IN THE DISTANT FUTURE.

"...We know he's time-travelling. We just don't know how he's doing it," the Time Guardian announces.

"Well, he's been lucky enough not to have caused a *time-warp* or *split*, which would make the Time-Flux unstable," announces his colleague.

"He's obviously chanced upon a secret key to the universe as we did hundreds of years ago. A *machine* of some kind, perhaps?" speculates the first Guardian. "And it obviously sends him on the same roller-coaster ride throughout the vastness of *space* and *time,* as does our machine, or so it seems. He's definitely addicted to it too, of that there's no doubt, otherwise he'd stop, because it's not a pleasant feeling shooting through a wormhole at the speed of light."

The second Guardian nods. "Yeah, feels like your body's being microwaved – a horrible, hot, sickly feeling. But by the endless readouts, this traveller's Time Machine seems to be the most advanced computer of its time – super-intelligent and super-sophisticated, besides being fantastic beyond belief in every manner possible. It seems to open up a whole new way of looking at time-travel. The Tunnel-Vortex he uses to transfer matter across the ages is so quick that he emerges almost instantly elsewhere. However, it must be a traumatic experience, because the readouts are extraordinary! Off the chart! We need to find him and stop him, but he always manages to stay under the radar, so to speak!"

***

BACK IN THE PAST, in London, at 130 Redwood Road, the O'Shea home, a big comfortable house with mullioned windows, Rory and Ben are in the front bedroom practicing their boxing skills – and they are making quite a racket while doing it.

"Rory! Ben! You're shaking the whole bloody house to

pieces, stop it!" shouts Ivy, Rory's mother.

"Oh, leave them be. I wish I was their age, I'd be up there with them," says Rory's father, Peter.

"But they're making a hell-of-a-row!" snaps Ivy.

"And that's why all children should be born girls," says their coloured maid, Hettie May Brown.

"If they were all girls, there wouldn't be any children at all, would there, Hettie?" says Peter with a wry smile.

"Rory, Ben, come down and get some dinner this instant!" Ivy shouts impatiently, banging on the ceiling with Hettie's broomstick. "Everything's ready and getting cold!"

"Okay," comes Rory's voice.

"Okay dokey," comes my younger-self's voice too.

They come trotting downstairs, cheerfully, into the parlour singing, "When Irish eyes are smilin'..."

The family dog barks, its ears flattening back.

"That dog has no appreciation for music and no taste!" say Rory and Ben in unison. And they say it every time the Red-Setter barks.

"Sit down, the both of you, and get your dinners," says Ivy. Rory shakes his head. "I've eaten, mum."

"Well, I haven't and I'm starving," says Ben.

"Come here, Hettie May, and let me check out your beautiful dumplings!" shouts Rory cheekily, and he chases her playfully around the table and out of the parlour door.

She snatches the broom from Ivy's hand as she goes. "You lay one Goddamn finger on me, my boy, and I'll swipe you with this!" she snaps, breathlessly.

"I'm in love with *you* and there'll be a full moon out later tonight!" announces Rory, laughing and giggling like a five year old.

Hettie May dashes for the back door. Rory slaps her backside playfully, then chases her all around the house shouting 'Yippee-ki-yay' while *she* screams.

Meanwhile, I watch my younger-self sit down at the dinner table with Mr. and Mrs. O'Shea. "Boy, oh boy, another good meal in the O' Shea household," he says, helping himself to a large plateful of stew and dumplings. It smells delicious.

Ivy looks exhausted. "My blood pressure will be through the roof before today is over," she says with a sigh, watching Rory chase Hettie May around the house.

Peter dishes out a generous helping of stew and dumplings for himself and Ivy, and Rory finally joins them at the table. "I hope you have a good journey, Rory. We're all going to miss you around here," Peter says with a tone of sadness.

"What's the matter, Pop, you look tired?" says Rory. "I'm going to miss you all too."

"Oh, had another run-in with old man Peabody today," says Peter. "I thought by making him a director of our company he'd ease up on us a little bit, but he's getting worse by the day."

"What is it with that mean, old, skinflint anyway?" Rory asks.

Peter shakes his head in dismay. "Oh, he's a frustrated old man with a sick mind," says Peter. "He has no spirit, no humanity and no soul, and he despises anyone with something he can't get his hands on – that includes us too."

"Nothing ever changes around here, does it?" says Ivy.

"I suppose you've already chosen your path in life, Rory?" says Peter

"Yes, Pop, what we've always talked about. I'm going to design and build things, plan modern cities and such, when I've done travelling."

Peter smiles. "Still chasing that first million pounds before you turn thirty, eh?"

"I'll settle for half of that in cash," says Rory.

"I would too!" says Ivy with a nod.

Peter chuckles and then his face hardens. "You wouldn't consider coming back to your old job at the loan company would you Rory?"

Rory's face hardens too. "Well, I... I..."

"I know, it's too soon to talk about it, but..."

"No, Pop, I couldn't come back, I just couldn't," interrupts Rory with a pinched expression. "I couldn't face being cooped up in that dusty, old office for the rest of my life."

Peter wipes his lips with a napkin and sighs.

"Oh, I'm sorry, Pop. I didn't mean it that way," says Rory. "But it is a penny pinching business trying to stay one step ahead of Mr. Peabody, which is impossible because he owns everything including the banks."

Peter sits quietly, eating his meal.

"I love you, Pop, and would do anything for you, you know that, but I'd go crazy in that poky office," says Rory. "I want to get out in the world and do something big, something really *important!*"

Peter looks hurt, stops eating, wipes his lips with his napkin again and picks up his wine glass. He takes a small sip of white wine. "You know, Rory; I feel that in some small way we are doing something important. We're satisfying a fundamental need for the little man because most people, even the ones without much money, want to own a home with cozy carpets and curtains, a bright blazing fire and a solid roof, and we're helping a lot of people to get those things even though we're in our shabby little offices," says Peter.

Rory looks ashamed. "I know, Pop, I know that. And I wish I thought the same way and could help. But I've been saving like a miser in order to travel and I just feel like if I don't get out of this town now, I never *will!*"

Peter nods sympathetically. "Yes, yes, you're right, son."

"You do see what I mean, don't you, Pop?"

Peter nods again. "Yes, this town is no good for anyone unless they're willing to crawl on bended knees to Peabody, and you've got a talent, son. You go and get out of here while you can."

"Pop, you want to know something? I've always thought of you as a great man, and you are, and everyone knows it including Mr. Peabody, which is why he feels threatened by you."

Peter smiles.

Then, Rory sees Hettie May listening in to their conversation at the dining room door. "Did I speak loud enough for you to hear all of that, Hettie, or do you want to come in and pull up a chair?"

Hettie jerks and pulls away from the door. "I heard it! And it's about time one of you young 'uns said it!" she announces, walking off into the kitchen.

Both men laugh.

"Boy, I'm going to miss her," says Rory. "Pop, I think I'll finish up here, get dressed and go for a drink with Ben if that's okay?"

Peter nods. "Have a good time, son. Your mother and I will clear up the dishes. Just don't go getting into any fights!"

Chapter 4
SOMEWHERE IN THE DISTANT FUTURE.

"...For years we've been searching for this particular Time Traveller, not knowing who he is or where he originates from. He leaves his signature resonance behind when he leaps, but it's so faint that it's positively untraceable. We may need the help of the Time Police to catch him," says the Time Guardian.

His colleague nods. "I'd love to know *why* there is only a faint residual trace of him left behind when he leaps. I do, however, realise there's more to this than meets the eye."

"The Time-Corridor he propels himself through, whether it's a Worm-hole or a Black-hole, must absorb most of his initial energy, leaving only the faintest traces behind. It doesn't even show up on the X-Ray Spectrogram and that's highly unusual, unless he travels the ages as a Sub-Atomic Particle Beam, which is only theoretically possible and has never been tried before," speculates the Time Guardian.

"I know," agrees his colleague. "The only actual clue to his time-travelling antics, and indeed his existence, is the faint ripple left behind when he leaps. It's like a flat stone skipping across a still pond."

The Time Guardian shakes his head, stiffly, searching the many computer readouts staring him in the face. "I need answers to my questions: How has he remained at large for so long? Is anyone of an extra-terrestrial origin helping him? Does he use the same power source that we do? If so, how much and how often? Is someone else protecting him from detection? And does he think he can keep on propelling himself through the centuries forever without consequences? Because there are *always* consequences!"

***

BACK IN THE PAST, Rory and Ben walk out onto the Old Kent Road, heading for the Genevieve Nightclub. They arrive and pay to get in after a five minute wait in a small queue. A live band is playing Soul and the music is very upbeat as they enter. Patrons are dancing, chatting and celebrating because it's Friday and the beginning of the weekend.

"Excuse me! Excuse me!" says Rory, forcing his way through the mixed crowd of drinkers, drunks, druggies and dancers. He notices two girls and waves, pushing his way towards them with Ben following.

"Well, well, if it isn't the, *soon-to-be-famous*, explorer and city builder, Rory O'Shea," says Julia with a glowing smile. "Did you fly in on your magic carpet?"

Rory smiles back at her. "I thought I'd come along and give you ladies a treat, by letting you see my dancing skills again," he announces for all to hear. "Besides, I want to see how the new pool turned out. I designed it to go under this dance floor."

Pete Tyler, the nightclub owner, strolls over looking like an over-stuffed chair in his new black suit. His smile is positively beaming from ear to ear. He grabs Rory's hand, shaking it. "Welcome to the new Genevieve," he says. "And anything you require is on the house tonight."

Rory nods cordially. "Thanks, Mr. Tyler. How's business?"

"Putting the pool under this dance floor was a great idea. In fact, it was a stroke of genius. People from all over come here to swim in the day now and dance through the night. Saved me building a whole new wing," says Mr. Tyler. "Enjoy the evening and have lots of fun tonight."

Another voice from behind welcomes Rory to the dance. He spins around. "Isobelle? Isobelle Hirst?"

Isobelle Nods. "Yeah, it's me."

"Well, by the look of things, it's old home week," says Rory, "and all of the old gang are here."

Everyone shakes hands, smiling at each other, and Julia's

pushed aside.

"Do me a big favour, will you, Rory?" says Isobelle.

"What's that?"

"You remember my sister, Emma, don't you? Dance with her."

"Me? Well, I don't know, I was just going to dance with Julia," says Rory looking around. But Julia's gone.

"Oh, go on, just one dance; do me this favour will you? She's always looked up to you," says Isobelle. "Just one dance and you'll give her the best night ever."

"I'm no wet nurse, Isobelle," says Rory. Then his jaw drops open as the crowd parts. Emma's standing, smiling at him admiringly. And she's stunningly beautiful with long dark hair and bright blue eyes. Voices are chattering all around him, the music is upbeat and loud, and almost everyone is dancing, but all that fades away into the background as Emma's gorgeous smile lights up the room, captivating him. Now, he only has eyes for her. He seems frozen for a moment, unable to move. And he can't take his eyes off her. Nor she him.

"You remember Rory, don't you, Emma?" says Isobelle with the shortest introduction ever.

"Well, well, well, what do you know?" says Rory. His arms circle her waist and they start dancing.

"Hey, it's my turn to dance with Emma!" says a newcomer.

Rory glares at him. "Oh, why don't you go away and annoy someone else!"

"Well, I'm sorry," says the newcomer looking embarrassed.

"You should be!" says Rory.

"Hey, wait just one minute, I'm not the one cutting in!" protests the newcomer. However, Rory and Emma dance off into the crowd.

"Well, hello!" says Rory.

"Hello," replies Emma. "You've a surprised look in your eyes as if you've never seen me before."

"Well, I haven't."

"You pass me on the street nearly every day."

"Who me? No, no, that's a little girl I used to know named Emma Hirst. That's not you!"

She smiles. "A little girl who grew up into a *woman*."

Suddenly, a klaxon sounds and my younger-self jumps up onto the stage like a Jack-in-the-Box. "Oh yez, oh yez, oh yez! Attention! It's time for the dance contest to begin!" he announces.

The whole gathering cheers.

"And the first prize is a staggering two hundred pounds," continues Ben. "Anyone *not* tapped on the shoulder by a judge will remain on the floor. Are you ready? Okay then, let's go!"

Instantly, the music changes from Soul to the roaring sounds of Saturday Night Fever and everyone takes to the dance floor.

"I've been practicing this, but I'm not very good," says Rory.

Emma smiles, shrugging. "Me neither!"

"Okay then, what have we got to lose?" says Rory, and they begin to watch and copy everyone else in the room. They click their heels, throw out their legs and arms and spin on the spot while dancing hand in hand, and they're really quite good.

Rory smiles at Emma. "Hey, you're terrific!"

They strut, Travolta-like, around the floor doing improvised moves, until everyone seems to be watching them. Meanwhile the judges circulate between the couples, tapping the weakest dancers on the shoulders, eliminating them from the competition – until very few are left.

Rory and Emma, however, are dancing up a storm until he

stumbles momentarily, catching his elbow on the lever mechanism which opens the dance-floor.

The two halves begin to grind inward silently towards the walls, exposing the pool beneath. Neither notice the floor opening up behind them and they carry on dancing. The crowd gasp and scream, trying to warn them of the impending danger – but they're enjoying themselves so much that they think they're being cheered on.

"Hey, we must be good!" says Rory breathlessly.

There are more gasps and screams, but they continue to dance until finally the inevitable happens – they plunge into the swimming pool and carry on dancing in the water as if nothing has happened.

***

"Night fever... night fever..." sings Rory as he and Ben walk Emma home in the moonlight.

"Night fever... night fever..." chorus Emma and Ben too.

"Holy cow! What a night, eh?! And I thought I'd be bored and go home early. Boy, you should have seen the commotion in that cloak room. I had to pick a lock to borrow those ridiculous dry clothes for the both of you," says Ben.

Rory's wearing a red and white striped shirt, baggy brown pants and no shoes. Emma's wrapped up in a long black overcoat that's touching the ground. And except for the overcoat, she's completely naked underneath.

"Do I look as funny as you do?" she asks.

"I guess I'm not quite the baggy pants type, am I?" he says.

"But you look wonderful, Emma, really."

She does a little curtsy. "Why thank you, kind sir."

"You know, if I wanted to say one thing about you, I'd say you were the prettiest girl in town tonight," he offers.

Ben shakes his head. "I'm heading home now before you Two love-birds decide to embarrass me." My younger-self turns, waves and heads on home with purpose in his stride, not wanting to play gooseberry.

She stares at Rory admiringly, longingly, lost in his voice, wanting him to kiss her. She's yearned for a single kiss for a long, long time. "Well, why don't you say it then?"

"Ok, I will! You're the most beautiful girl in town, and not just tonight, but every night!" he blurts, colouring red in the moonlight. "Hey, how old are you anyway?"

"Nineteen," she says.

He gives a snort and chuckles. *"Nineteen?* Then last year you were only eighteen!"

"Am I too young for you?" she inquires, gazing up into his bright eyes.

"Oh, no, no. You're exactly right. I like the ring of *nineteen*." he said enthusiastically. "But you certainly look older without your dress on. I... I mean without your clothes on. I mean younger. You look... well, just... oh, I don't know *what* I mean." He accidentally treads on the hem of the overcoat.

"Uh-oh," she says.

"Ooops, I'm on your..."

"Yes."

"Ooops!"

"Sir, your clumsy foot is on my coattail," she announces quietly.

He stares down. "Oh, a curse upon me for being a clumsy oaf. I shall remove my size nine from your caboose m'lady." He picks up the hem of her overcoat, passing it to her.

"You may kiss my hand if you wish," she says, holding it up to him.

He stares at her beautiful face, framed by the moonlight. "Hmm. Hey. Hey, Emma," he mumbles softly, wanting to kiss her lips more than anything in the whole wide world. He leans in close.

She feels awkward and slightly embarrassed, pulling away.

"Oh, I see," he sighs. "Okay then, I'll throw a rock at the old Hennessey house!" He picks up a stone the size of a cotton reel, pulling back his arm, ready to throw.

"No! No, don't! I love that old dusty house, even if it is derelict!" she says.

"You don't understand. If you can hit the door, you can make a wish," he says, struggling to hold up his pants with his free hand, the pants being at least three sizes too big. "And you have to be a *hell-of-a-good-shot* from here!"

She shakes her head, grabbing his wrist. "Don't Rory; it's a romantic old place, even though it's dusty and falling to pieces. I'd love to live in it someday."

He stares at the house. "In that place? It looks haunted. I wouldn't live there if I was a *ghost.* Here watch this; I'll throw this stone right through the letterbox." He lets fly and there is the sound of shattering glass. "Ooops! Hit the window instead!"

She stares at him. "What will you wish for?"

He turns and stares into her shining eyes. "A whole hill full of wishes, Emma. I know what I want to do tomorrow, and the next day, and the next week, and even next year, because tomorrow I'm saying goodbye to London and I'm going to travel the world like I always planned to. Africa, India, Greece, Italy and anywhere else I can get passage to. And then I'm coming back and I'm going to learn how to build things. Extraordinary things. Cities. Skyscrapers and the longest bridges."

She looks deeply hurt. His plans don't include her at all. She picks up a small stone.

"What will *you* wish for?" he asks.

She doesn't answer. She does, however, throw the stone

and hits the door.

He's impressed and smiles at her. "Wow, Emma, that was a pretty good shot. Did you make a wish?"

She doesn't answer. Instead, she begins singing, "Night fever... night fever... we know how to do it. Here I am... waitin' for this moment to last..."

"Come on, Emma, what did you wish for?"

She shakes her head stiffly. "Not telling!" She carries on singing.

"Come on, tell me?"

She shakes her head again. "If I tell you, it won't come true."

In the moonlight, she'd never looked lovelier. "Come on, Emma, what do you want? A star? Say the word and I'll throw a lasso around one and pull it down. You want the North Star?" he whispers in her ear.

She smiles sweetly. "I'll take it and wear it on my finger like a diamond ring."

"Am I talking too much, Emma?"

Suddenly, a man's voice rings out from a nearby house, startling them both. "Yeah! Why don't ya kiss 'er instead of talking 'er to death, ya great ape?"

Rory stares at the man in an upstairs window across the street. "How's that?" he shouts.

"Well, are ya gonna kiss 'er, or do ya want me to come an' do it for ya?" came the voice again.

"You want me to kiss her, huh?" says Rory.

"Oh, why is *time* wasted on the young," shouts the man, slamming his window shut.

"Hey! Hey, you! Hold on mister! Come back out here! I'll show you a kiss that will curl your hair!" snaps Rory.

Suddenly, a car screeches around the corner and comes to a jarring halt. Uncle Thomas jumps out. "Rory, come on home quick! Your father's had a heart attack!"

Rory can't believe his ears. "What? Is he okay?"

"The Doc's with him now," says Thomas looking pale.

Rory's shaking and pale now too. He turns to Emma. "I'm sorry, I've got to go. Will you be okay?"

She nods. "Go, quickly, I'll be fine!"

"Come on, let's hurry," says Thomas.

Rory climbs into the car. "Go Uncle Thomas!"

Chapter 5

The Time Machine stops the proceedings again. Suddenly it seems to become pensive, its gears and mechanisms clicking away in thought. "Peter O'Shea's sudden death shocked everyone, not only at the Loan Company but in the whole community around Redwood Road. One moment he was a loving husband, father, friend and contented business man, and the next... he was dead. His funeral was attended by family and friends only, but the whole community mourned his passing as a tragic event. He had been well-liked and treated as a local hero by the poor folk of London, because every time Mr. Peabody reared his ugly head, to put up the rents on his ramshackle properties or foreclose on a mortgage unfairly, Peter came to their rescue like a knight in shining armour."

"Oh, dear. How did Rory take his father's death?" I ask.

"Not too good," replies the Time machine. "See for yourself. This is one month later at the board meeting of the Loan Company to decide its fate."

***

Tea is being served, drinks poured and sandwiches passed around on paper plates as Rory casually appraises the board of directors in their dusty office surroundings that smell of mildew and age. The walls are lined with bookcases, crammed full of books with the odd space for a cheap reproduction painting or two. The floor is wooden and devoid of polish. And the hushed topic of conversation is the fate of the O' Shea Loan Company.

"Peter O'Shea was a man who inspired and demonstrated great affection for his company and his fellowmen, but now he's dead and the fate of the company hanging in the balance because of one man, Mr. Peabody, a horrible, tight-fisted old man with greed in his watery eyes. He is a thoroughly unlikeable man, sharp tongued and wily and constantly digging for scandal and prying for gossip to underpin his deceitful schemes against the Loan Company," says my Time Machine.

***

"...I think that concludes your business here, Rory," says the Chairman of the Board nodding sadly and speaking somberly. His fingers dip into his waistcoat pocket, bringing out a silver watch on a delicate chain. "I know you're in a hurry to catch the Kensington and we have a taxi waiting for you downstairs right now. I just wanted the board to know that you gave up your trip to Europe in order to straighten out your deceased father's affairs here. So, good luck to you on your travels."

"Good luck, Rory," says the whole board in unison, except for Mr. Peabody.

"And now we come to the main purpose of this meeting, to appoint Peter O'Shea's successor," says the Chairman.

Mr. Peabody signals for his aid to push his wheelchair closer to the meeting table. "And I'd like to get to the reason for my being here... to dissolve this company," he announces in a loud voice.

"Now you just wait one minute," says Uncle Thomas.

"Wait for what?" asks Mr. Peabody. "I've come to say *my* piece and it's this. I say this company was one man's pipe-dream, Peter O'Shea's, and now he's dead it isn't necessary in this town any more. Therefore, Mr. Chairman, I make a motion to dissolve the Loan Company!"

"Peabody, you despicable old skinflint, I'll wring your..." snaps Uncle Thomas.

"Order! Order!" says the Chairman. "It's too early to talk about such things. It's only been a month since Peter died and more time is needed to sort out the financial affairs and dealing of the Loan Company."

"Well, I second Mr. Peabody's motion to dissolve the company," offers one of the other directors. "A month's long enough."

All of the board members begin arguing and bickering amongst themselves about the fate of the company, but the Chairman uses his gavel to bring the room to order. "Oh, very well," he says looking angry and confused. "In that case, I'll ask Rory to withdraw and we'll put it to a vote. But I'd like to express the deep sorrow of the whole board at the passing of Peter O'Shea. Thanks for coming." He shakes Rory's hand.

Rory stands up. "It was my father's dream to create the Loan Company. He was solely responsible for its organization and I'd like to think that to the public he was an institute that became the Loan Company."

"Peter O'Shea was *not* a business man," interjected Mr. Peabody. "He was a dreamer and that's what finally killed him." *Not a great loss,* his mind echoed. "Oh, I don't want to sound harsh or disrespectful, because he was a man of good character, but he had no common sense and was ruining this business. Just take this last loan to Arnold Bishop, a lorry driver. I happen to know my bank turned him down as a bad risk, but he came here and we granted him a loan to build a home. Why?"

Rory turns, clearing his throat. "Well, I handled that deal, not my father," he says, staring angrily at Mr. Peabody. "You have his paperwork there, his salary, his insurance, and I can personally vouch for him."

"An associate of yours, eh?" says Mr. Peabody with a sneer.

"Yes, Sir," answers Rory respectfully.

"This is my whole point gentlemen," says Mr. Peabody. "Just because some of us drink and watch football with this rough rabble, they shouldn't be able to come in here and borrow our money." He chuckled evilly. "Lending money to these discontented, lazy good-for-nothings will only see us go broke. We should be lending money, if at all, to the thrifty working class. Now I vote to..."

Rory slams his fist down hard onto the meeting-table, staring venomously at Mr. Peabody. "Now, just you wait one minute! Hold it right there! My father *was* a dreamer and no business man, I know that, and why he ever dreamed up this company I'll never know. But neither you, nor anyone else has the right to blacken his good name!"

Mr. Peabody shakes his head. "Up until a month ago, this town had *one* too many dreamers, but now Peter O'Shea's gone, the Loan Company should go too."

Rory stares hard at Mr. Peabody, unable to believe what he's hearing. "My father, God rest his gentle soul, helped a lot of people to get out of your flea-ridden slums, and that's the only reason you want to dissolve this company. Well, you men are all shareholders, aren't you proud that we've helped make better citizens by lending them money and building them decent homes? Because I sure as hell am!

"If the good people of London had to wait and save their money for a home, none of them would have a roof over their heads now because it takes years to save that kind of money. Just remember this, Mr. Peabody, the rabble you're talking about do most of the hard work, and they live and die here in this neighbourhood. So, is it fair to have them do it without a solid roof over their heads? My father didn't think so, and neither do I. They're human beings with families, for God's sake, and should be treated as such – not treated like so many cattle."

Mr. Peabody slams his hand down onto the table, looking mean and moody. "I'm not interested in what you think!" he snaps hardheartedly. "I'm only interested in *my* share of this company, and as a director I request that it be dissolved today!"

Rory stares at him even harder. "You're not interested because you're not *human.* And you have no *feelings* because you have no heart and soul! You're a pathetic, frustrated, shell of a man and to my way of thinking my father died a hero in everyone's eyes, except yours, and a much richer man than you'll ever be!" Rory is agitated and shaking now, his voice almost high pitched.

"I vote to dissolve this company," says Mr. Peabody. "And there's nothing you can do to stop me!"

"I know what your problem is. You've never been able to get your dirty hands on this company while my father was alive and it galls you!" snaps Rory. "Well, he's dead and I've... I've said too much already. I..."

"Our town needs this broken down institution even more than ever now," interrupts Uncle Thomas.

Rory nods. "You're the *Board of Directors.* Do what you will with the company, but for God's sake do the right thing, and not what Mr. Peabody would have you do. There is just one more thing though. Uncle Thomas is right! This town *does* need the Loan Company more than ever now, if only to have somewhere to go to borrow money or get a mortgage instead of crawling on bended knees to people like Mr. Peabody. Come on, Uncle Thomas, let's go!"

Uncle Thomas stands up, glaring venomously at Mr. Peabody, and both men leave the room with the whole board of directors arguing amongst themselves.

"Boy, oh boy, that told him, Rory old chum," says Uncle Thomas picking up his overcoat from the back of a chair, putting it on, buttoning it up, finally wrapping a scarf about his neck. Rory did the same, listening to the Chairman banging his gavel in the next room, trying to restore order to the meeting.

"What happened in there?" asked Tilly. "I heard a lot of yelling and shouting."

"Mr. Peabody is voting us out of business after thirty years of blood, sweat and toil, that's what," says Rory, madness in his eyes. "Guess I'll get going now before my ship *sinks*."

"Yeah, you better hurry or you'll miss it," says Uncle Thomas looking at his watch. "Taxi's waitin'."

"Boy, it's gone really quiet in there. Wonder what's happening?" says Rory, looking like he's forgotten something.

"Don't fret yourself about it, it's not your concern anymore," says Thomas. "They're puttin' us out of business. But, so What? Go on, before you miss your ship. The world at large beckons!"

"Doesn't it bother you that you're fifty-five years old Uncle Thomas and might not get another job?" asks Rory.

"Yeah, but it'll bother you more if you miss the Kensington and your trip around Europe," smiles Uncle Thomas.

Suddenly, a loud voice comes from the Board Room. "Rory! Rory! They've voted against Mr. Peabody!" says the Chairman, bursting through the door. "They want to keep the company going!"

Rory, Tilly and Uncle Thomas cheer and hug each other.

"You did it, Rory. You changed their minds," announces the Chairman. "They do have one condition though."

"Only one?" says Rory, his eyes fever bright. "What is it?"

"They've appointed *you* Executive Secretary, to take your father's place," says the Chairman.

Rory's face hardens and he squirms. "Oh, no, they can't do that. Uncle Thomas is staying on, but I'm leaving. I'm not missing my trip to Europe. Uncle Thomas's your man, not me."

The Chairman shakes his head. "But, Rory, they'll change their vote and go with Mr. Peabody if you don't take the job, and as Executive Secretary you can hire anyone you like, including Thomas."

"I'm going to Europe. I'm leaving right now and I'm going to travel. This is my last chance!" snaps Rory. "I missed out because of my father's death, but I'm not missing out now. Uncle Thomas's your man, not me!"

"Rory, Mr. Peabody will win and get his way if you don't stay and take the job," says the Chairman.

***

The Time Machine stops the proceedings again, its gears whining and clicking, the city lights outside dimming slightly then brightening again.

"He didn't go to Europe, did he?" I say to the Time Machine.

"That's right. Rory ran the Loan Company for a whole year, waiting impatiently for the day when his Uncle Thomas was capable of taking his place as they'd agreed," says the machine. "And today's the day. Plus, Rory's brother, Michael, is coming home from the army where he saved the lives of twenty men on patrol in Afghanistan in a raging fire-fight against overwhelming odds. Watch, listen and learn, because if you're to shape Rory a new future, where he doesn't decide to commit suicide, you will need answers to all of his questions when you meet again as a Time Traveller in his past!"

***

BACK IN THE PAST.

"...Are there lots of jobs for people who want to travel?" asks Uncle Thomas, fingering the train timetable to see what time Michael will arrive.

"You don't have to take my word for it. Just look at these

advertisements in the Sun Newspaper," says Rory. He reads them out loud. "Construction worker wanted in Venice. Oil worker required in Texas. Man with engineering experience wanted in Panama. The list is almost endless and goes on and on, Uncle Thomas."

Suddenly a whistle sounds, startling them and a train comes rumbling around a bend in the track. It shudders to a halt. Steam hisses and puffs in ragged geysers from beneath the wheels and the engine, and several doors slide open. Passengers disembark hurriedly, smiling and whistling merrily, one of which is Michael.

"Here he is," says Rory smiling broadly, shaking his brother's hand, giving him a big hug. "Michael O' Shea. All hail the English hero!"

"Why, if it isn't my would-be explorer brother," says Michael. He turns to face Uncle Thomas. "You haven't aged at all," he announces, shaking his hand too.

Uncle Thomas smiles. "We've all been too busy to get old, you know."

"Oh, boy, are we glad to see you," says Rory. "And you're on time for a change. Mom's at home cooking the fatted-calf in your honour, you son-of-a-gun. Come on, let's go eat."

"Oh, wait. Wait a second. Rory, Uncle Thomas, I want you to meet Ann," says Michael. He turns, pulling a beautiful redhead to his side. Ann feels herself blush and sticks out her hand quickly. She nods. "Glad to finally meet you both."

"Hello!" greets Rory, shaking her hand gently.

"Well, how do you do?" says Uncle Thomas.

"This is Ann Lake," announces Michael.

"Actually, it's Ann O' Shea now if you don't mind," she offers, colouring red.

Rory hesitates momentarily, his face hardening. Then his

jaw drops, hanging wide open. He's stunned by the news.

"I wrote you to say I had a surprise in store, and here she is!" says Michael.

Uncle Thomas' face beams. "Well, how about that. Your brother's a married man!"

Rory nods and doffs his baseball cap. "Well, glad to meet you. Congratulations to you both," he says with an awkward, hesitant smile. And the awful truth is – that he's scared. He's waited a long time for his brother to return from Afghanistan, and his duties in the army, to take his place alongside Uncle Thomas at the Loan Company. *Has that changed now too? Am I to be stranded in London forever like my father was?* he wonders.

"Come on, Mrs. O'Shea, I can't wait to see the look on their mother's face when you tell her the good news," says Uncle Thomas, pulling her along, arm-in-arm.

"What's a beautiful young woman like you doing getting hitched to a penniless bum like my brother?" Rory asks playfully.

"Well, he won't be penniless for long, because my father's offered him a job," says Ann.

Rory's face hardens again. He stops dead in his tracks. "Oh, he's got a job too besides marrying you?" he says, staring icily at her. "Is it a package deal?"

Ann blushes and says nothing more. She just carries on walking with Uncle Thomas, leaving Rory and Michael behind. Rory, however, looks distraught, his feelings hurt. He's wasted another year of his life helping to run the O' Shea Loan Company.

"Rory, about the job I've been offered, Ann shouldn't have mentioned it because I never said I'd take it," says Michael. "You've been holding down the fort here, long enough. I won't let you down. I... Oh, wait a minute... I've forgotten our bags. Back in a jiffy!" He turns, running back to their carriage and disappears inside.

Rory's rooted to the spot, thinking. His brother's future seems set in stone as far as Ann's concerned. Whereas his own aspirations to travel, explore the world and build great things seems to be sinking deeper into the mud by the second. Everything he's ever dreamed of doing seems to be fading away fast. He stares at Uncle Thomas and Ann, who have stopped to look in a sweet-shop window on the platform. His legs feel heavy, like lead, and they disobey him at first, but finally he moves alongside them both. He taps her gently on the shoulder and she turns to face him. "Yes, Rory?" she asks.

"Er, er, Ann. This job. What is it?"

"An I.T. job in New York," she offers. "Michael's a whiz with computers and such."

"Is it a good job with lots of money?"

"No, not much money to start with, but it definitely has a secure future, because my father feels he's the right man for the job. In fact, he's so taken with Michael and his skills, he feels he's the *only* man for the job. Now isn't that perfectly wonderful?"

Chapter 6

The Time Machine's laser-light-show stops in freeze-frame. I stare solemnly at the image in front of me. It's a picture of the O' Shea household and a gathering of family, friends and guests from the local community, all singing, dancing and making merry in the parlor, celebrating Michael's marriage to Ann. And it looks like there isn't a single person who doubts whether he has made the right choice for a wife. Ann seems to be the perfect host, besides being the perfect woman. She is elegant, charming and witty, besides being beautiful.

Now I stare out of the living room window. Rain is lashing the London landscape and the wind howls like a banshee, distracting me momentarily. "How much more of Rory's life do I need to see before I'm ready to go back to 1987?" I ask.

The Time Machine's gears and cogs seem to race away in thought. "Not much more. But what I'm showing you is relevant and it's vital that you know everything there is to know before I propel you back to that fateful night when Rory takes his own life. Keep watching, listening and learning."

***

BACK IN THE PAST, Rory and Uncle Thomas are out on the porch, toasting everything from marriage to the moon and both are intoxicated, particularly Thomas who's feeling rather fine. "Oh, boy, I feel great! I feel so good that I could go and kick Mr. Peabody in the ass! In fact, I think I will!" He burps richly.

Rory wafts the air in front of him. He smiles. "What did you just say? That was in my bad ear."

"Oh, maybe I'll do it tomorrow," says Uncle Thomas looking around. "Where's my hat? Where's my...?"

"Here it is!" says Rory, plucking it from Thomas' head.

He holds the hat out in front of him.

Uncle Thomas stares at the hat, seeing three of them. "Thanks, but which one is mine?"

Rory smiles at him. "The one in the *middle*."

Uncle Thomas takes the hat from him and puts it on. He shakes Rory's hand. "Oh, thanks. Boy, oh, boy, I feel dizzy. Point me the way home, if you will."

Rory nods, turns Thomas to his left and points. "That way, down there."

"Boy, oh, boy, what a great night," says Uncle Thomas.

"Just turn this way a little more and follow the path for two hundred yards, then turn left and you're there," Rory instructs.

"Oh, that way, huh?" says Uncle Thomas blinking hard. He shakes his head too, trying to lose the dizziness swamping his mind. Then off he wobbles down the path singing, "Show me the way to go home... I'm tired and I wanna go to bed..."

Rory laughs at the sight, shaking his head in amazement. He turns to go back inside the house, but then as he climbs the three wooden steps there is a loud crash and the tinkle of breaking glass from somewhere down the path. He spins his head to the sound.

"I'm alright! I'm fine! I'm alright, really!' shouts Uncle Thomas.

Rory laughs again and goes inside, shaking his head, listening to Uncle Thomas cursing colourfully. Then Thomas begins to sing again as he winds his way home. A train whistle suddenly blows in the distance. It's the 9:15 Express Train and it makes Rory feel melancholy. He places his hand inside his deep coat pocket and pulls out a handful of travel leaflets he's collected over the years. He fans them out. Among them are tours to South America, including Brazil, Uruguay and Argentina. There's also tours to New York,

New Zealand, Egypt, Germany and Paris. It makes him feel trapped and even more melancholy. He stares at them for a long time. Then his mother appears from out of the parlor looking for him. His face hardens and he sighs, secretly dumping the leaflets in the waste bin. "Hello Sweet," he greets.

She puts her arms around his waist, kissing him on the cheek. "That's for being you," she whispers. "How do you like Ann?"

Rory forces a smile. "Oh, she's lovely isn't she?"

"Looks like she can keep Michael under control," she says.

"Keep him away from the O'Shea Loan Company too," he snipes, biting his tongue.

"Did you know that Emma's back from college?" she asks.

"No, I didn't."

"Came back today. Lovely girl, Emma. The kind of girl who might help you find answers to the questions you've been asking yourself all these years, Rory."

His face softens slightly. "Hmmm?" he grunts.

"Give me one good reason why you don't call on her and take her out?"

"Because she already has a boyfriend. That's a pretty damn good reason, isn't it?" he offers. "And Charlie's *crazy* about Emma."

His mother frowns. "Yes, but she's not crazy about him. She's in love with you. Always has been."

"Well, just *how* would you know that?" asks Rory.

His mother kisses his cheek again, staring at him lovingly. "Because I have eyes and ears. She comes alive and sparkles like a jewel whenever you're around."

"Oh, she does, does she?" he exclaims, colouring red. "Hogwash!"

"Besides, Charlie's always away on business. And you're

here, *alone* in Redwood Road, and all's fair in love and war isn't it?" she says with a pout.

"But Charlie's a good friend of mine, mother."

"But he's an absent friend. And *always* away!"

Rory laughs. "*Mother* you're so transparent. I see right through your plan. You're trying to marry me off too!" He kisses her on the lips and gives her a gentle hug.

She takes the baseball cap from his hand, placing it firmly on his head.

He laughs again. "Oh, my hats on my head now. I take it then that I'm in a hurry? Well, okay chum, old pal of mine, I think I'll go for a walk and find someone to do a little passionate kissing with."

"Rory, do yourself a favour, be serious and go see Emma."

"Well, mum, I'll have you know that I am serious, so point me in the right direction."

She turns him towards the door, giving him a gentle push.

"That direction, eh? Then I'll bid you a good night, Mrs. O'Shea!"

She opens the door and gives him another gentle push. "Good night *Mr. O'Shea!*" she says, closing the door behind him.

***

One hour later, on the Old Kent Road, Rory is eyeing up the local talent. Pretty girls are passing him by as he walks on past the brightly lit shop windows, decorated with Christmas baubles. The girls are all smiling at him as he whistles merrily and carries on walking towards the Genevieve Nightclub, when who should come walking towards him in the opposite direction.

"Well, hello there Rory," Julia greets.

"Hi Jules!"

"What're you doin' tonight?"

He smiles. "Nothing much. Just out for a walk."

"Where to?"

"Oh, I don't know," he tells her. "You got any plans for this evening?"

"Nothing at all," she says with a wink.

"Then, what are we waiting for? Let's make a night of it!"

"Okay, what shall we do?" she asks excitedly.

"Well, let's go out in the country and walk through the trees," he says. "Then we can go and sit by a waterfall in the moonlight."

"Huh?" she murmurs looking confused. She stares at him, perplexed. She expected him to say something completely different like, "Let's go for a meal, or a dance, or a drink in a Nightclub."

"Then we can swim in a pool and play with the fish..." he continues.

"Rory, stop! Are you completely nuts? I don't want to walk through trees or sit by a waterfall in the moonlight, and I certainly don't want to go for a swim with fishes. If you think I do, you're crazy!"

He looks confused. He's trying to be romantic. "Oh, okay, let's just forget the whole thing then! Guess it was a bad idea anyway!" he snaps, and he storms off down the busy street.

She stands with her mouth hanging open, watching him go, not knowing what to say or do.

No more than five minutes later, he's pacing up and down the pavement outside Emma's home, looking beside himself. He's irritated and agitated by Julia's offhand rejection of him. Suddenly, Emma appears at an upstairs window.

"What are you doing, Rory?" she shouts.

He spins around, looking up. "Oh, hello Emma, I was out for a walk and just happened by."

She smiles. "Yes, so I see. Well, have you decided yet?"

"What?" he asks.

"Whether you're coming in or not. Your mum rang to say you were on your way here."

"Mum called you? But... but I didn't say I was coming over here for definite," he stammers.

"Mmmm, well, maybe not, but you're definitely here."

He laughs. "I sure am. What are you...?"

She disappears from the window and he begins pacing up and down again. She runs downstairs, stopping briefly to fix her hair in an oval mirror as she goes. She picks up a music tape and places it in the tape deck, turning it on. It begins playing, *Night Fever*. Then she opens the door, watching Rory pacing up and down the pavement. "Well, are you coming in or not?" she asks.

He stops and stares at her. "Well, okay, I'll come in for a little while," he says, trying to open the catch on the top of the gate. "But... but I can't seem to..." Finally he kicks the gate open out of pure frustration and marches down the shingle path towards her. "I really didn't tell anyone I was coming over here, you know."

"If you say so, Rory."

"No, really!" he protests.

"Okay, it's no big deal, Rory," she says, looking at him through puppy-dog eyes.

"She loves saying his name, and it rolls off of her tongue with relish. She has been in love with him from the very first time she'd set eyes on him in school," announces the Time Machine suddenly.

I listen, but say nothing.

Rory stares at her standing in the doorway, back-lit from behind, and she looks like an angel. "Wow, where did you get that wonderful dress?"

She smiles sweetly. "Do you like it?"

He smiles back at her. "I wouldn't have said *Wow* if I didn't."

She stands aside and he steps into the front porch, his neck craning and twisting, unable to take his eyes off her, enthralled with the way she looks, and he never even notices his favourite dance music playing on the tape-deck. "Didn't expect you back from college so soon," he says.

"Well, Charlie's in Scotland working and I was homesick," she replies, staring up into his smouldering dark eyes.

"Homesick? For London? Are you completely nuts!" he says with a sneer. "I've been trying to get out of this *mad-house* forever!"

She stares at him solemnly. "I know you have. You've had some really bad luck these last few years, what with your father's untimely death and Mr. Peabody's devious efforts to undermine the Loan Company. But my heart is here with..." She stops herself from saying – *you!*

"You're so right about my bad luck. If I didn't have bad luck, I wouldn't have any luck at all."

"Would you like to sit in the lounge and talk?" she asks, staring up at him like a lovesick child.

"Oh, okay, just for a minute or so."

She leads him into a brightly lit, comfortable room with a pair of glass doors leading to a veranda, over which is a pergola covered with flowers. "Okay, sit here," she gestures, touching a cushion on a long beige couch. He sits and she sits by his side, facing him.

He sighs as he removes his baseball cap. "This is a nice room, Emma. It smells wonderful too, like pine needles. Love that smell." He feels guilty for being there while his friend, Charlie, is away. Charlie is, after all, Emma's fiancé.

***

SOMEWHERE IN THE DISTANT FUTURE.

"... Sir, we have a temporary fix on the rogue Time Traveller. He's currently in the year 2012, but so far we haven't managed to acquire a stable grid reference for his actual whereabouts," says a Time Analyst.

"How do you know it's a 'He' and not a 'She'?" asks a Time Guardian.

"Because *He* leaves a faint male pheromone trace as he leaps through the Fourth Dimension. It's barely detectable and hardly traceable, but it's definitely male Sir!"

"Then it should only be a matter of *time* before you lock onto him, and then I want him eliminating before he can change anything else. Definite ripples are being beamed across the centuries and I want him eradicating before he causes the unthinkable to happen! Find him at all costs! Or the Space Time Continuum will simply cease to exist, along with the whole universe!" says the Time Guardian, his voice deep and harsh.

***

BACK IN THE PAST.

"...I heard about your brother getting married, Rory." The words roll off Emma's tongue with a certain relish again, the magic word being *marriage*. "That must have been quite a surprise."

"Yeah, quite a surprise. Quite a *big* surprise actually, for the whole family."

"Do you like his wife?"

"Oh, yeah, she's a doll. But I never imagined that Michael would settle down this soon. He's still so young."

"What about you, Rory? Can you see yourself getting married and settling down soon?" she quizzes, hoping he'll say *yes*.

"Good Lord, no! Heaven forbid!" he says. "Marriage is okay for the right people I suppose but..."

Just then the telephone rings, interrupting him, before he can finish answering. Emma stands up and turns the music off. She swings around and picks up the 'phone from its cradle, placing the receiver to her ear. "Hello?" she says with a sudden irritation in her voice. Rory's rejection of marriage now swamps her mind and she can't seem to think of anything else. "Hello, who is it? And why are you calling at this late hour?" she snaps.

"Hello my Sweet," a man's voice says at the other end of the line. "Were you asleep? It's not really late you know, it's only 9:00pm.

"Charlie?" she says, feeling suddenly dispirited.

Rory climbs to his feet on hearing his friend's name. He puts his baseball cap back on, feeling even more guilty for being there. But Emma doesn't want him to leave. In fact, she's desperate for him to stay.

"How're you?" asks Charlie. "Are you okay?"

Emma shakes her head to clear her mind. "Yes, yes, I'm fine," she replies after a long pause.

"It's so good to hear your voice again, sweetheart," says Charlie, his tone low and controlled.

Emma stares at Rory, who's heading for the front door. She clears her throat noisily. "Charlie," she says, "there's a friend of yours here, Rory O'Shea. He's come to call."

There's a palpable silence for a moment on the other end of the line. "Rory's there?" comes the reply finally. "Put him on!"

Charlie wants to speak to you," she tells Rory, handing him the receiver.

Rory stares at her. "Me?"

She nods.

He takes the receiver from her and puts it to his ear. "Hello," he says, his voice a quiver.

"Well, well, a fine friend you are! What're you trying to

pull? You trying to steal my girl while I'm away?" says Charlie, his voice angry and loud.

"What do you mean?" Rory asks. "I'm not trying to steal anything, including your girl. Here, talk to Emma, she'll tell you I'm just leaving." He's passing her the receiver when Charlie's voice screams down the line, "Hey, wait a minute, you!"

Rory puts the receiver back to his ear, and Emma is so close to him that she can hear every word her fiancé is saying.

"Look, I have a big business deal going on here," Charlie says in a stern voice, "and it's going to be a month or so before I can get back home, so I don't want to find out that you two have been doing something behind my back! I'm going to be rich soon and then we're going to be married see!" Charlie's voice is so high pitched and agitated that he's almost hoarse.

Emma looks up into Rory's face longingly, soulfully, rejecting Charlie's words in her mind. She doesn't want to marry him. She wants to marry Rory. And always has. She only started a relationship with Charlie to try and make Rory jealous, but it hasn't worked.

Charlie's cold, harsh words ring in Rory's ears as he stares down into Emma's fever bright eyes. Her beautiful face is framed by the lamplight. And for the very first time he sees her as he has *never* seen her before. It's as if a fog has been lifted from his eyes. She *is* beautiful. Very beautiful. And her lips are getting closer and closer to his. Now they are almost nose to nose. But then suddenly, Rory stops and pulls away.
Now he stares at her as if he doesn't know her and has never seen her before. And then he shakes his head. He puts the receiver back to his ear and Charlie is still rambling on about his business affairs, saying that he has Emma's future all mapped out. Rory puts the speaker to his mouth. "Aww, shut up prattling on will you, Charlie!" he snaps, slamming the

receiver down onto the hook. He places the telephone onto the sideboard and grabs Emma by the shoulders, pulling her close.

"What am I doing? You almost had me under your spell there for a moment," he says. "But you're Charlie's girl, so listen to me. I don't care if I *am* in love with you. I don't want to get hitched, ever. Not to anyone. Do you get that? I want to do what I've always dreamed of doing. I want to travel. Go to far off places. Design and build things. And I want to do what I want to do – not what you or Charlie do or don't want me to do. And I'm not changing my plans, now or ever. Not for any..." He stops suddenly.

Emma shakes her head at his outburst, looking horrified but not surprised because his plans to travel and build great things have been thwarted at every turn. Instantly, she's overcome by a horrible, stomach-twisting feeling that this night has somehow been inevitable. She begins to cry. His harsh words cut into her heart like a flaming dagger.

"And you're... you're..." he begins again. But then he stares hard at her, watching her crying. It tears at his heart. And the more he gazes into her eyes, the closer his lips come to hers again – as if drawn by some unseen force. Suddenly, the blood seems to rush to his head and his cheeks flush. Now he has the overpowering urge to kiss her. And he can't stop himself. So he does kiss her. Then he kisses her again passionately. And again.

Now they fall into each other's arms and they kiss over and over, making love. Mad, passionate, wild love that seems endless, heady and euphoric. And all of his plans and schemes fade away for the few hours they are joined as one. And he finally realises just how much he does love her. "Oh, Emma, Emma, I'm so sorry for making you cry earlier." He pulls her closer, holding her tighter, until she can hardly breathe. He kisses her forehead. Eyes. Nose. Cheeks and lips.

"Oh, Rory, Rory," she whimpers, breathlessly, "I love you, and always have..."

Chapter 7

SIX MONTHS LATER.

"...Here they come! Here they come! The happy bride and groom!' shouts the whole gathering in unison as the Wedding March sounds out. Everyone cheers, throwing rice and confetti at Rory and Emma. They stop and kiss. The crowd cheer louder.

"Have a great honeymoon Rory! You too Emma! And God bless you both!" a woman's voice shouts as they make their way through friends and family towards an awaiting taxi. Some are laughing, some are crying, but everyone is cheering the bride and groom, shouting, "Good Luck!"

Rory and Emma finally reach the taxi and climb in as it begins to pour with rain. The whole gathering groans at the sudden change in weather, but they still throw their confetti and yell their good wishes. Rory's mum is standing, waving, with Hettie May. "First it was Michael's turn to get married and now Rory's," she says, looking wistful.

"We're just a couple of old maids now," volunteers Hettie May.

"You speak for yourself," says Rory's mum, laughing.

Meanwhile, the newly-weds speed off towards the train station and they are still kissing and cuddling in the back of the taxi.

***

The Time Machine stops the proceedings in freeze-frame again at a picture of Rory collapsed in a shadowed doorway, looking like a down-and-out drunken recluse. He's unshaven, malnourished and looks positively ill. "This is a picture of your friend five years after his wedding to Emma, and now comes the really important part of Rory's decline and why he decides to take his own life. He gets into debt, to the tune of

£50,000, while trying to stave off Mr Peabody's attempts to dissolve the O'Shea Loan Company. His house is being repossessed too because he hasn't paid the mortgage for over a year. He's drinking heavily, to the point of becoming an alcoholic, which is why his wife, Emma, leaves him and takes the kids to live with her mother. Plus it looks like he's going to jail for misappropriating company funds.

"And as if that's not bad enough, he believes he's worth more to his family dead, rather than alive, because he has a £100,000 life insurance policy with Emma as the only beneficiary. Now you know why your best friend commits suicide, so you have to figure out how to convince him that things aren't as bad as they seem – even though they *are!*"

"Well, for-warned is for-armed but I still have no idea how to go about this task," I admit.

I set the dials on the Time Machine for the Tower Bridge in London, at 11:55pm, on Christmas Eve in 1987 and hit the button. Suddenly, there seems a breath of wind in my flat but there are no windows open. The lights are switched on and flicker once or twice as if there's a power surge. Then the room becomes indistinct and my reflection in the mirror looks hazy, *ghostlike,* flickering in and out of sight. Everything is silent for a moment as my reflection vanishes completely from the mirror. There is a loud click, a dull drone, and my mind reels from the mad feeling of falling weightless through *time.* I black out momentarily, but when I come back to my senses I feel my body weight return and I am there on Tower Bridge. Rory's there too – near the middle.

I stand watching him. He's shivering, preparing to throw himself off the bridge into the freezing black water of the Thames River. It's snowing heavily and I'm chilled to the bone because I forgot to put on my heavy grey overcoat. So, God knows how Rory feels in his thin shirt and lightweight suit.

It looks like he's praying, then he crosses his heart, climbing up onto the top railing, getting ready to jump. What do I do? Do I shout to get his attention? Do I say, "You can't jump, it's against the law!" Or do I run over and restrain him, or walk calmly over and try to rationalise with him that what he's doing is wrong and against God's law?

I reason that the latter is the best option and begin to walk over without him seeing me. Clumsily I trip over something. I lose my balance, hit my head on the railing and go flying over the side, heading for the water, screaming like a lunatic. "Help! Help! Help me, please! Arghhhh! Then I hit the freezing water like a brick and it numbs me instantly, disorienting my senses.

It's ice cold! And the next thing I know, Rory jumps in after me and swims me to the safety of the muddy bank side, where he drags me out of the water, gasping for air like a grounded fish.

"You alright mate?" he asks, water dripping everywhere.

"Yeah. But I thought I was a goner for sure," say I.

Suddenly a man comes running over from the bridge gatehouse, shining his torch onto the both of us like a huge spotlight. His eyes widen and then narrow in a squint, trying to see more clearly. "How the hell did you manage to fall into the Goddamn water?" he asks with a lisp. He stares hard at me.

I stare back. "I tripped, fell and hit my head when I saw this guy getting ready to kill himself," I say. "Then *he* saved me."

"Well, I didn't go through with it and kill myself, did I?" announces Rory.

"It's against the law to commit suicide, particularly by launching yourself off Tower Bridge. You can go to jail for it, you know," the gatehouse man states dumbly.

I laugh at the man's ridiculous remark.

Rory laughs, seeing the funny side too.

"Hey, Rory, you've got a cut on your lip," I say.

"Yeah, I got smacked in the mouth by a piece of driftwood when I jumped in the river to fish you out, mister. Hey, how come you know my name?" says Rory.

"Oh, I know all about you. In fact, I know everything there is to know," say I.

"Have we met before?" asks Rory. "You look kinda *familiar*."

"I knew you when we were twelve."

"Well, who are you then?"

"Ben Ward. Your best friend!"

"Bullshit, mister, Ben's the same age as me and you look fifty years old if you're a day!"

"I *am* Ben Ward. And I'm a Time Traveller too."

The gatehouse man looks at me like I've escaped from a lunatic asylum. "Right, I've heard about enough of this crap. I'm callin' the police and they can sort the two of you out!" He does an about turn and heads for the gatehouse door, marching as if his next step might bring him to his nose. I watch him disappear inside.

"Oh, boy, that's a corker!" says Rory with a laugh. "A Time Traveller, eh? Well, why are you here then?"

"Because it's not worth killing yourself over money, not even £50,000," say I.

"And just how do you know about the money?" he asks looking staggered. "There's only two people who know how much I owe, besides the police, me and a certain Mr. Peabody."

"I've just told you, I'm a Time Traveller and I know everything about you, up until what happened tonight," say I.

"Well, if you've come here to help me, have you brought

£50,000 with you?" Rory asks with a sneer.

"Oh, no. No. I haven't got that kind of money, but I'll think of something."

"Well, don't worry yourself about it, 'cause I'm worth more dead than alive," Rory snipes.

"Now look here, you mustn't talk that way," I chastise. "I'll think of something, and everything will be fine. You just don't realise how much you've done for this community and how much they care for your welfare."

"Yeah, if it wasn't for me, everybody'd be a lot better off. Especially my wife, kids and friends," says Rory. "So go back to the future, or whatever lunatic asylum you're from and leave me alone, will you?"

I stare at Rory, holding my chin in my hand. "Oh, this isn't gonna be easy. So, you think ending it all would make everyone feel better, eh?"

"Yeah, or maybe it would have been better if I'd never been born at all," Rory replies in a whisper.

"What?"

"I said, I wish I'd never been born."

"Don't say that! You... Hang on a minute. That's not a bad idea! Yeah, that might convince you!" I say.

I take out the Time Machine and punch in Rory's relevant information: age, size, weight and so on and so forth, down to the minutest detail. Then I click onto 'SPECTRAL' and press the 'GO' button hesitantly. The machine buzzes and vibrates in my hand. "There you are," I say. "Now neither of us exist anymore, or so it will seem to the outside world."

"What are you rambling on about, you nut?" Rory snaps.

"For all intents and purposes, *we* don't exist in the present *time period*. Neither of us. So you haven't a care in the world. Because if you don't exist, you can't owe £50,000 to anyone. The police will eventually stop looking for you. You're wife and kids will get your life insurance money because you've gone missing without a trace – and everything will be fine," I tell him, smiling inside.

"That's it! Enough of this bullshit! I need a stiff drink!" announces Rory. "Either you're insane, or I am for listening to you!"

Rory stands up and takes a step back away from me. "Hey, my clothes are bone dry," he says. "But I was wet through two seconds ago."

"You don't exist anymore, so how can you clothes be wet?" say I.

"Hey, I can hear in my bad ear too."

"Like I said, you don't exist so things have changed for the better, which is what you wanted."

"Oh, I don't understand what's happening here so follow me. I'll buy you a beer in the nearest bar and we'll talk about it," says Rory holding his head in his hands. "Well, come on whoever you are, I'll buy the first round."

No more than five minutes later, we're walking into a scruffy looking joint, full of cigarette smoke and it stinks of sweat. I pull a sour face. "Looks like a real dive."

"Well, I know the owner and he's a friend of mine," says Rory. "Come on, we'll have that beer."

I shake my head, saying nothing, walking to the nearest table where I sit down. Rory heads for the bar and leans on it, trying to get the barman's attention without success. "Hey you! Hello! Look, I'm standing here waiting!" he says.

The barman stares in his direction, but then carries on serving everyone else. Rory leans further over the bar, waving at the barman. "Hey, what's the matter mate, are you blind besides being deaf? Can't a thirsty man get a drink around here?"

The barman walks his way.

"About time too!" snipes Rory

But the barman serves the customer by Rory's side and walks off to the other end of the bar, lighting a cigarette, where he puffs away merrily.

Rory turns and stares at me blankly. He makes his way through the rough looking clientele back to where I'm sitting. "Can't seem to get a drink in here for love nor money," he says loudly. "The barman just ignores me!"

I look up into Rory's face. "That's because he can't see you. No one can. Not in here, or out there. You don't exist in this time period, remember?" I tell him flatly.

"Hogwash!" he says.

"It might seem hard to swallow, but it *is* the truth. My machine and the laws of physics have given you a unique opportunity – to see what the world would be like if you'd never been born!"

"Bullshit! What are you, a mind reader? A hypnotist? That's it, you're a hypnotist and you've done something to me!" snaps Rory.

"I'm a Time Traveller, plain and simple," I say. "And you and I are now on a Spectral Plain, unseen and unheard. So why are you complaining? You were the one who didn't want to be born, didn't want to exist. Well, I've granted your wish and you'll see and hear a lot of strange things from now on."

"Oh, yeah, well if I don't exist, how come I can slap you silly," says Rory swinging an arm in my direction.

He tries to hit me with an open handed slap and his hand passes right through my face. He tries to hit me again. And then again, until he looks exhausted. "What... what have you done to me?" stammers Rory looking horrified.

"I'm doing what no other person on earth can do for you. I'm showing you what *your* life is worth to the community. For instance, if you hadn't stopped Mr. Fowler from sending

The poisoned prescription to the Ramsey family, all those years ago, he would have spent his life in jail for poisoning their boy, and you would have been implicated and become a jailbird yourself. Don't you see, I've given you a great gift, Rory, a chance to see what the world is like without you."

Rory shakes his head, trying to clear his mind. "Now wait just one minute. This must be some sort of hallucination. Goodbye whoever you are, I'm going home!" He stands and marches to the door, then turns to stare at me ponderously.

"Even if you go home, no one can see or hear you," I say.

Chapter Eight

As Rory heads for home, dim shadows of his surroundings are always looming somewhere in the background for him to hear, see and smell, but not touch or taste in his Spectral Form – but he doesn't understand the concept. Now it begins to snow heavily and the flakes pass straight though his body and fall onto the ground. It's unnerving and disconcerting for him to see this happen, and even more disconcerting when he sees that he has no reflection staring back at him from a lit shop window. Panicking, he begins to run and keeps running for a long time.

It's snowing heavier now. Finally he stares at the sign in front of him, covered in icicles, welcoming him to Redwood Road. Bells are ringing and most of the town's residents are singing on the side-walks as he strides down the tree lined streets decorated with shining fairy lights and glowing lanterns.

He walks on past the old Emporium, the Bank and the crowded shops to get to the brightly lit homes, and as the singing fades into the background he comes to the O'Shea family residence where his mother still resides with Hettie May Brown. His mother's talking to a neighbour on the doorstep. Rory rushes up the shingle path and stops directly in front of her. "Mother!" he says, his voice trembling. "Mother, listen please! Something terrible has happened to me, please help me! I don't know what it is, but it's strange and scary! Please help me until I get over it!"

Rory's mum carries on talking to her neighbour, completely unaware of her sons presence there.

"Mother, I need your help! Please!"

***

SOMEWHERE IN THE DISTANT FUTURE.

"...Sir, the Time Traveller has begun giving off a heat signature, but strangely there's *two*," says the Time Technician.

"A heat signature can only mean one thing," says the Time Guardian. "His machine has *Spectral Form* capability, which is similar to invisibility when travelling. You say there are two signatures?"

"Yes, some yards apart. Which means there are *definitely* two entities and not a single split signature."

"Track them both and get me a fix. And let me know the instant you have!"

***

"...Mother, it's Rory, can't you hear me? I'm here, look, take my hand!" He tries to touch her, but can't. His hand simply doesn't exist in the same time-period. "Mother, for God's sake, what's happening to me? Something's happened to everybody and I'm alone! Please let me stay with you until I'm over whatever it is!" Fear is shining in his eyes. A great fear of the Unknown.

She finishes her conversation and goes inside, closing the door in Rory's face with a slam. Now he's realising that what I've told him is true, and that I haven't cast some sort of spell over him. And he finally understands that each man's life touches and affects so many other lives.

I walk up to him, making him jump. "You see, Rory, you haven't had such a bad life after all. And your life touches so many others. If you hadn't been born, Mr. Fowler would have gone to jail for a long time and your brother Michael would have broken through the ice and drowned at the age of twelve, instead of going on to fight in Afghanistan where he got a medal for saving the lives of every man in his company. You see what a mistake it would be to throw your life away?"

"Where's my wife, Emma, now?" Rory asks.

"She's still at her mother's house with your kids," I tell him, and he races off in that direction. I watch him go, shaking my head. "For the love of God, she won't be able to see or hear you!" I shout. And then I follow in his footsteps, but there is no crunching sound in the thick snow. Just an eerie silence.

After a ten minute forced march we arrive at Emma's mother's house. The lights are on, but no one seems to be home. Rory peers through each downstairs window in turn, craning and straining his neck to see inside. "Emma!" he shouts, trying to knock on the window-panes. But his hand doesn't make contact with the glass. It slips straight through silently. He shouts and shouts. I hear him. No-one else does.

"Where is she? Where's Emma? Where are the kids?" Snaps Rory, staring at me mad-eyed.

I tell him. He doesn't like the answer. He tries to hit me. "You're a liar! Now do whatever you've got to do to change things back to how they were before we met! I want my life back as it was!"

I take out the Time Machine, turning the dial away from Spectral and click the button. Instantly, my body-weight returns. I can tell that Rory's back too. Snow is settling on his head and shoulders instead of passing through him. He licks his cut lip.

"Hey, I can taste blood again!" he says with a grin.

"Of course you can. Everything is as it was, and I hope I've made you see what a mistake it would be to throw everything away," I tell him. And just as he's realising what a mistake it would be to throw away his life, a police car comes bowling around the corner, screeching to a halt at the curb and two burly officers jump out.

"We've been lookin' for you all evenin'!" says one.

Rory's eyes widen. "You can see me?"

"Of course we can! And we've a warrant for your arrest!" says the other.

"You can hear me too? Then arrest me and get me the hell away from this lunatic," says Rory pointing at me.

They bundle him into the car and speed off with Rory shouting, "Merry Christmas" over and over, while I'm left with my jaw hanging wide open, watching it all happen. I have to think fast. What to do next?

***

At the police station, Rory is being interviewed, by the Bank Examiner, about the missing money.

"Mr. O'Shea, there's a deficit of £50,000 in the Loan Company funds. Can you explain why?"

"Isn't that just the damnedest thing! Looks like I'm going to jail, doesn't it? Can someone call my wife and tell her that I'm alive and well, anyway," says Rory with a grin, "even though I'm a captive in this draughty old Police Station?"

"Is that all you have to say?" asks the Bank Examiner scratching his head.

"Mister, an hour ago, I was going to kill myself over the missing money because my home's been repossessed. My wife's left me too, taking my kids away. I've also become an alcoholic and my life's a complete mess and in ruins – but the worst *you* can do to me is put me in jail! And the funny thing is, I have no idea what happened to the money, because I didn't steal it in the first place! Now can someone please call my wife and tell her that everything will be okay when I've straightened things out?"

***

Meanwhile, I'm searching London for Emma. I know what she's doing and know Rory wouldn't like it, but hey, he's in jail with no 'Get-out-of-jail-free' card – so hard luck.

Finally, I find Emma and follow her all around London

and she is persistent and relentless in her endeavors, until she is exhausted and looks like passing out. I approach her and tell her that Rory has been arrested and we both head for the Police Station.

When we arrive, Rory stands up and kisses Emma on the lips and she reciprocates telling him that she's never stopped loving him, but can't handle his constant drinking. He swears his undying love for her and says he won't touch another drop. The next moment, Uncle Thomas comes bursting through the doors with two black plastic bags. "It's amazing how many friends you have Rory! So many! Emma scoured London telling everyone that you were in trouble and they all went out collecting money without asking *why*? I've never seen anything like it! It was like watching an army of ants roaming the streets!"

More people burst into the Police Station in one's and two's, donating even more money. Then, the arresting police officers search their pockets and throw what little money they have onto the huge pile of notes. "Merry Christmas, Rory!" they say, smiling broadly. "And there's more money on its way by the look of it!"

Rory is dumbstruck by the amount of cash piled high on the Sergeant's desk. "God bless you all!" he says with misted eyes and a lump in his throat.

Eventually, after twenty minutes or so, there's about two hundred people crammed into the room and each one has a small bag of money to add to the growing mountain of cash. Even the Bank Examiner contributes with a smile. Then Mr. Fowler comes through the doors with a goldfish bowl full of money, followed by Tommy the taxi driver with his nights takings. Both men smile at Rory and dump their cash on the desk with the rest of it.

Hettie May comes bowling through the doors next and

contributes. So does Rory's mother. Then Emma's mum arrives with Rory's two children, Olivia and Errol, who place a Santa sack full of money down in front of the Bank Examiner and pull funny faces at him. Now everyone laughs, cheers and shakes hands, exchanging Christmas greetings. Emma's in tears . But they're tears of joy.

"I wouldn't have a nice home if it wasn't for you Rory!" shouts one man.

"Me neither, if it wasn't for The Loan Company and you Rory!" says another. And another. And another.

"Quiet everyone! Quiet! Quieten down a minute! I have an email to read. It's from Scotland," announces the police sergeant. "It says: *I know we've had our differences over the years, but we've also been best friends for a lifetime. I'm sorry to hear you're in trouble, Rory, so I've posted you a cheque for £10,000 from my company funds, which the Loan Company can repay when it gets back on its feet. I know you'd do the same for me. Merry Christmas pal!* It's signed Charlie."

Emma sheds more tears of joy. Rory picks up Olivia and Errol, one in each arm, loving, hugging and kissing them, and everyone begins singing Christmas carols as the Bank Examiner counts the pile of money. Paul screws up the warrant for Rory's arrest and throws it in the waste paper basket.

Now I smile as Rory's brother Michael comes through the doors wearing his Army uniform, decorated with several medals. "A lot of people owe you so much, brother, including me. You saved my life when we were kids, and because of that I was there to save my army buddies in Afghanistan."

Everyone cheers. And now that my mission of mercy is over, I quietly write a short note and place it in Rory's coat pocket before setting my Time Machine for the present day in London and my cozy flat. Then I drift off, watching myself disappear from the mirror above the Sergeant's desk. I smile, thinking about the words in the note.

Dear Rory, life is definitely worth living when you have so many friends and loved ones, don't you think? Have a good life! I signed it: *your friendly neighbourhood Time Traveller, Ben Ward.*

Oh, and as a matter of consequence and coincidence, Mr. Peabody was arrested later that same day for the misappropriation of The Loan Company Funds. *He* went to jail instead of Rory. Poetic justice – don't you think? And being a lawyer myself, I love it when the Justice System actually works and puts the bad guy away!
  Okay, I admit it, I did leave the evidence for the law to find. But he *was* guilty after all!

Chapter Nine

In the present day, it's a cold Christmas morning. I open my cards and the first one is from Rory and his family, wishing me a happy festive season. I smile to myself wistfully. Knowingly. Well, I managed to do the impossible and actually stopped him from committing suicide, changing the past once again without even causing a ripple in *time*.

I walk to my wall bar and pour myself a Glenlivet with a splash of water. Then I open more greetings cards and there's so many. I think about Rory and how many friends and loved ones he has. He's a lucky man. He kept his promise too. He never touches a drop of alcohol any more, and I know because I visit the family regularly and they are stable now and so, so happy together.

I take a large swallow of my scotch and open more cards. I think how lucky I am too, to have so many friends. However, I have realised what a fragile existence we lead in our day to day lives, and it's amazing how many risks we take on our journey through life. Even simple things like crossing the road can be fatal in the blink of an eye. I mean, you don't have to climb a mountain to fall to your doom – a twenty foot ladder can be just as deadly. But life does seem to combine all the ingredients needed to make our journey fun-filled, like a brilliantly imagined story, if we take the right path.

Well, take me for instance, I was a boring, do-gooder lawyer until two years ago and now look at me – I'm a Time Traveller for Christ's sake, and my power seems almost limitless. I can visit the past or future, spend as much time as I want there, and almost no time has elapsed in the present day when I come back. I can even *freeze* time if I like, for short periods. So now I catapult myself through time at every opportunity, and even though the journey risks my life time and again, I just can't help myself.

I've seen myself being born. I've seen myself die. I've even seen the world end and it's a frightening sight and an awesome spectacle, but nothing else seems to give me the thrill I seek and make my heart pound and my pulse race like travelling through the Fourth Dimension.

Now I look out at the London lights and the city is lit up like a vast Christmas tree. I stare at my watch. It's 9.00pm and time for another scotch and water. I place the Christmas cards around the room in order of size and walk to the bar, filling my empty glass. I sit on the couch, wondering where and when I should propel myself next? And for what purpose? Then suddenly I'm aware that the whole room is trembling and my vision is blurring, when a man comes running through my living room wall like a ghost with a gun in his hand. It happens so fast that I'm frightened. I smell something funny, feel an electric shock and drop my glass to the floor. I pass out.

***

I come back to my senses, sometime later. I'm sat on a chair. My hands are tightly bound and I'm gagged. A very bright light is shining in my eyes and I can't see a damn thing. I blink hard, several times, but it doesn't help. I hear voices, but can't tell what's being said. Someone slaps my face twice. Once with the palm of his hand and then once with the back of it.

"Ah, finally, you're awake," a voice announces. "I thought I'd killed you with the shock-gun." Someone takes the gag off. At first I thought the voice said shotgun, but then my mind clears and 'Shock-Gun' rings in my head. The bastard, whoever he is, hit me with a Taser and the darts are still in my chest and sting like hell.

"That must have been quite a jolt you gave him, it's taken him the best part of three hours to come to his senses," a second voice says.

Now I realise I'm naked and freezing cold. "Who the fuck are you guys?" I ask, my voice a quiver. "And what the fuck do you want with me?" My pulse is in the red zone.

"Your troubles have only just begun," announces the first voice.

I'm slapped about the face again, then punched in the mouth, cutting my lip. I cry out. "Why are you doing this, you bastards? Who are you?" I'm punched viciously again, repeatedly.

"You're an illegal Time Traveller," says the second voice. "For which the penalty is death. But we want to know who gave you the Time Machine in the first place. So, who was it?"

By now my head is spinning from the slaps and punches and I can't think straight, but I can taste the blood in my mouth from my cut lip. Suddenly the blinding light is switched off and an old man with a badly scarred face, wearing a blue robe wanders casually towards me with his arms folded and his hands in his sleeves. He reminds me of a monk, but without the hair missing from the crown of his head. He comes face to face. Nose to nose.

"You *will* tell me what I want to know before we terminate you, make no mistake about that," he whispers with a sneer, looking mad eyed.

My mystery deepens. They obviously know who I am. But who are they? Even a Hollywood thriller writer would struggle to make up what's happening to me right now.

"Doctor, shall I give him another jolt with the Shock-Gun?" asks the first voice.

Doctor? Doctor who? None of this makes any sense, I'm thinking.

"No! I want him lucid and wide awake, knowing that his living nightmare *is* a reality!"

Where the hell am I? And when? I think. And then the guy in the blue robe answers me as if he's reading my thoughts.

"We are *Guardians* and *Historians* in your distant future, and Time Travel has been outlawed for centuries."

I stare at him, but say nothing.

"Ah, I see I have your full attention now," he continues. "Our future stems from your past, and whoever controls the past also controls the future. For that reason we do not allow anyone to travel through the Fourth Dimension without a licensed permit on government business, and only at a time of great need."

A hologram of a chart lights up in front of me. "What the hell is that?" I ask.

"That's a graph of your illegal time travelling activities," says the robed guardian, "and you have altered the flow of time on several separate occasions and been dangerously close to causing a Time Paradox that would cause *time* and the *universe* to cease to exist!"

The second Guardian steps in front of me too. Shit, he looks just like Samuel L Jackson, the film actor, only meaner! I shake my head, thinking I'm hallucinating from the pain of my wounds, but hey, his voice sounds just like him too!

"Who supplied you with the Time Machine?" he asks, his voice like ice.

He punches me hard in the face, cutting my eyebrow and blood seeps down into my eye obscuring my sight. I blink the blood away. "Is that the best you've got?" I ask. He punches me harder, splitting my top lip wide open. Blood drips into my mouth and I taste it again. *Guess I asked for that! No point telling them that I invented the Time Machine, they won't believe me anyway.*

I am now subjected to several types of brutal torture for what seems an eternity, and the pain is beyond belief. I hear myself scream over and over – animal screams – then I pass out.

When I come back to my senses, I hear the same voices talking to me.

"Ah, you're awake again. Good, we can carry on with our conversation," says the robed Guardian. "And your torture won't end until you answer my questions."

He punches me in the face again and I grunt.

"Tell me who's helping you Time Travel and who made the machine?" He punches me in the stomach. I grunt again.

"No one's helping me!" I scream.

"Did you think you could get away with your crime forever, Time Travelling without consequences? Go anywhere? Do anything? Because there are always consequences! Well we've got you now, so you can't use the machine anymore!"

I pant and struggle, watching the Guardians smile at each other with self-satisfaction.

"Prepare the lethal injection, he's not going to talk so why waste more time. We have his machine and that's all that counts," says the robed Guardian.

"You can't do this!" I scream, gasping for air, struggling with all my might to be free of my bonds and the chair.

The other Guardian prepares the injection. A lethal blue serum. He holds it up in front of me, taunting me, pressing the plunger slightly and it squirts like a miniature fountain. He smiles, leaning my way.

The numbness of terror creeps over me. "Don't do this!" I scream.

The robed Guardian turns his head staring at me with a mixed look of arrogance, pity and self-satisfaction.

Suddenly, I hear a loud humming sound and my chair begins to vibrate. The lights flicker twice, dim and go out.

Two laser like eyes shine in the dark. Something cold, made of metal touches my skin, freeing me. The lights come back on and there are several flashes of red and violet laser light that almost blind me and lay waste to the whole room. High pitched screams echo around the walls and the two Guardians vapourise right before my eyes, settling to the floor in two piles of dirty grey ash that smell of burnt flesh.

Nav-Man's awesome metal frame fully materialises in the blackened, charred room. And I have never been so glad to see him. "Freedom always comes at a price, Time Traveller, and the Time Guardians have just paid that price," his metallic sounding voice announces.

"I thought I was a goner for sure," I tell him.

Purposefully he clanks over to a far wall and smashes through it as if it were made of children's' building blocks. Sunlight filters through the huge hole in slanting shafts of rainbow coloured light and I smell grass, wet from the recent rain and hear birds chirping in the trees outside my prison wall. I stand up and shuffle to the hole, staring out. "This is the future whether I like it or not," I tell Nav-Man.

"Well, luckily, it's not where we belong and we won't stay a moment longer than we have to," says Nav-Man. "My understanding of this time-period is that terrific shocks, tension and death awaits any unsuspecting traveller. Therefore, we need to find your machine and get out of here as soon as possible. The Time Guardians have their eyes, ears and fingers into everything, everywhere, and have created a whole new *Space-Time* universe based around different sciences and future technologies, and the choice they have made is to make humans more aware that the Space-Time-Continuum is fragile and shouldn't be tampered with by anyone – particularly people from the past."

I nod. " I was under the impression that they are

international peacekeepers and not a military force, until they began torturing me. Now I realise that they are much more pro-active on the military side and were created to be co-operative, but deadly if necessary. Even their Time-Flux-Capacitors have morphed into mighty metal super soldiers, one of which is called *Praying Mantis* and is huge. I saw it earlier and heard them talking about it. It makes you look like the Tin Man from the old film, *Wizard of Oz*.

"You know, I often ponder the effects of time and time travel. I've changed my past life several times for the better, as in my boxing career and stopping Jane's murder, but has it had a 'Butterfly Effect', one where I've changed my life so radically that it has altered everything else for the worse, for those around me? Have I stopped people meeting each other that should meet and have a happy life with children? Has one small change in my past made a vast difference to the future of mankind? And I must admit, I'm not too sure of the answer because every time I return to the present, my mind snaps back and seems to acclimatise to the subtle changes around me, even if it has had a domino effect on the lives of others. In fact, everything seems to blend right in."

Nav-man nods with a clank. "I can follow most of the changes, but some are too subtle to notice."

Now I thrash around the smouldering ruins of the room, searching in drawers and cabinets for my Time Machine. I take a deep breath as I open drawer after drawer, but there is no machine to be found. *What the hell did they do with it,* I wonder?

Nav-Man watches my every move with his laser eyes, without moving his head, but his artificial brain is working overtime, clicking away in thought. "Super X-ray on!" he suddenly announces, and the whole room is illuminated with a strange blue light, revealing what is hiding behind every nook and cranny in the room, and inside every drawer or cabinet.

"I'd forgotten about you being able to do that," say I.

"I thought you had," gloats Nav-Man. And if he could smile, he would.

I imagine the impossible, living without the machine, when finally I find a drawer with my clothes in and dress quickly. My other belongings, including the Time Machine are with them too. I program Nav-Man to return to my flat in the present day and send him off. Then I set my machine for the same time and place and press the button, leaping the centuries, propelled by the law of physics. However, something is not right. I groan. "Ah.. damn!" My body feels red hot, like I'm being shrink wrapped, and I can't breathe. "What's happening?" I bang my knee on something. It hurts like hell. I can't see anymore. I bang my head and pass out.

***

Finally, I come to my senses. I rub my head and stare at the machine. The screen reads: Sunday, 18th June, 1815 AD. There are loud explosions and gunpowder flashes all around me; hundreds of men too in strange uniforms that I don't recognise. Most have a weapon of some kind in their hands and they're all yelling a strange battle cry in what sound like French, and I can understand it even though I never learned French at school. But how can that be?

The noise is unbelievable. Soldiers are running hither and thither, screaming. There are bodies torn apart by *grapeshot*; small pieces of metal, and legs, arms, heads and other bodily parts laying scattered everywhere like pieces of raw meat. The sight is beyond imagination or description and the stench of death makes me wretch. I look at the date again. Sunday, the 18th of June, 1815 AD. I stare at the surrounding countryside, picturing a specific page from one of my history books. The scene that forms in my head is similar. I look up at the sun and can tell it's early afternoon. I stare down at the ground and it's wet and muddy from the recent rain.

For the love of God! I think to myself. *I'm near Waterloo in Belgium, and I'm watching the Imperial French Army, under the command of Emperor Napoleon, being defeated by the armies of the Seventh Coalition, commanded by the Duke of Wellington, combined with a Prussian army. It's Napoleon's last campaign. His defeat here at Waterloo will conclude his rule as Emperor of the French, marking the end of his One Hundred Days return from exile.*

Suddenly, a musket is thrust in my face.

"Gotcha Frenchie!" an English voice announces.

I stare at the man, fear and fury bubbling inside of me.

"I'm not a Frenchman! I'm English, just like you!" I tell him.

"Cor blimy, guvner, I thought I had a Frenchie dead to rights?!" he states, shaking his head, looking me up and down, staring at my modern attire. "Them's seriously strange clothes yer wearin'!"

"Yeah, they're all the rage in America!" I blurt off the top of my head, not having any other rational explanation. "Who's in command? Who's your superior officer?" I ask.

"Why, Wellington of course. The Duke! He's up on yon escarpment takin' care of business."

"Can you get me up there? I need to speak with him urgently!"

The man nods. He turns, beckoning for me to follow and we squelch over the muddy ground, through the ranks of fighting soldiers engaged in hand to hand combat, and as I run, I'm shot at, almost bayoneted and narrowly miss being blown to smithereens when a huge crater opens up in the ground in front of me with the roar of cannon fire in my ears, but finally we make it to the escarpment.

The soldier I've been following approaches a princely looking man, wearing a short crimson tunic covered in gold braid at the shoulders and cuffs, plus crisp beige leggings and knee length, black boots. The two men speak in whispered tones for a moment and then the latter waves me to come forward. I approach very wearily as he stares me up and down.

"You are an Englishman?" asks Wellington with a look of suspicion.

"I am," I admit firmly.

"Can you explain your presence here and your odd attire?"

"I can't explain it in a way that would make any sense to you," I say. "But I can tell you this – your decisive engagement at Waterloo began on the 16th and will end on the 19th of this month of June. Napoleon has delayed giving battle until now to allow the muddy ground to dry, while your army is positioned here on the Brussels road on the Mont-Saint-Jeane escarpment, withstanding and repelling small repeated attacks from the French. This evening, the Prussians will arrive in force and break through Napoleon's right flank, and at that moment your Anglo-Allied army must attack and drive the French army from the field of battle!"

He stares at me with a look of suspicion. "Are you a fortune teller, sir?"

I shake my head stiffly. "No. I'm a *Time Traveller*, armed with the knowledge of what you must do to win this campaign. And if you do what I say, pursuing Coalition forces will enter France and restore King Louis to the French throne. Napoleon will then abdicate and surrender to the British. Later, he will be exiled to Saint Helena, where he will die in 1821."

The Duke stares at me again, like I'm a half-wit. "A Time

Traveller, sir? Do you really expect me to believe such nonsense? Admittedly, you dress rather oddly and appeared amongst the British ranks under strange circumstances, but do you really expect me to believe you're from the future and know what is about to take place here?"

"But it's the truth my dear Duke," I tell him.

He begins slapping his thighs, laughing with great gusto. "Well, I'll be a monkey's uncle. I've heard everything now!" he says. "Is it not rather a large thing to expect me to believe that your real existence is in the future, sir?"

"I arrived here this morning, quite by accident, when my Time Machine had a hissy-fit and propelled me through the Fourth Dimension to the *wrong* time and place, nothing more and nothing less," I say. "However, to prove what I'm telling you is true, I tell you this – as a part-time historian I know that your initial disposition this morning was to counter Napoleon's threat of enveloping the Coalition armies by moving them to Mons, south-west of Brussels. This in effect would cut your communications with your base at Ostend, but would also push your army closer to Blucher's. I also know that Napoleon manipulated your fear of the loss of your supply chain from the channel ports with false information from embedded spies. Need I go on? Or do you now believe I am a fortune teller and not a Time Traveller?"

Wellington scratches his head. "That's exactly what I *was* thinking when I woke up this morning, and I told no one. Goddamnit! How the hell could you know what I was thinking?"

I smile to myself faintly. "Now do you believe my story?"

He nods his head stiffly, eyes wide. "What will Napoleon and his forces do today?" he asks in a whisper.

I stare him squarely in the eyes. "He will *lose this battle,* because of the admirable resolve of the British army and

Coalition forces; because of the bad weather conditions and muddy ground, and because he doesn't attack in the morning and strike while the iron is hot," I tell Wellington as I put my hand into my deep coat pocket, producing my machine with its parts of brass, nickel and ivory, its size no larger than a calculator.

Wellington watches me reset it. I press the relevant buttons and drift off. My heart is beating fast, it's hard to catch my breath and the last thing I see before everything goes black and I pass out is Wellington's disbelieving gaze, staring at me. But he did take my word, thus winning Waterloo in style, as well he should after getting the best advice anyone could get in a similar situation.

Chapter Ten

Finally, after what seems an eternity, I return to the present day and my flat in London. I need a drink. I walk over to the wall bar and pour myself a scotch with a splash of water and down it in one large swallow. I pour another and down that too. I sit ruminating for a quite a while, thinking about my latest experience on the battlefield at Waterloo. I could understand the French language and every word they uttered, except for their war-cry. But why was that? I never had any French lessons at school. Then, I suddenly realise the truth of the matter and the only plausible explanation. The Time Machine must provide a complete, moment-by-moment, manageable language breaker, so that no matter where I am in the world – there is no language barrier. I certainly had thought of everything, it seems, when I tinkered the machine together in the future.

I have a sudden thought. *I can go anywhere in 'time', spend hours, days, weeks or months even, and then return to the present day and hardly a minute will have elapsed, but what if I can go to any country too, and speak their language with the help of my Time Machine – that's even more incredible. Had I really integrated this useful information into the machine's memory, so that I can not only understand any language, but actually speak it too? And the answer is: I must have.*

***

SOMEWHERE IN THE DISTANT FUTURE.

High chandeliers are ablaze with the light of a star. Men in white robes, wearing necklaces that pulsate around their necks, are speaking in hushed tones, sat around a large oval table made of an unknown alloy. The table pulsates with colour and speaks in a deep authoritative way, giving its opinion.

"You are all rising stars of the current political party, but when the cover-up threatening to shake our nations power structure is blown wide open, heads will roll! Billions of dollars are at stake and no one's integrity or life is safe until our current problem is resolved! Has anyone here got a reliable solution to put forward today?"

Shardlake the Enforcer nods. "I will go back in time and *kill* the son-of-a-bitch!"

The urgent meeting at the Global Time-Tunnel Council, traditionally held in secret, had been cancelled earlier because of the giant solar flares heading for earth and it had been too dangerous to assemble, but now the members of the Great Council were sat twiddling their thumbs, racking their brains for a solution to their problem. Shardlake's solution was heavy-handed and drastic to say the least, but probably appropriate and necessary in the whole scheme of things.

Salem, a thin-faced old man with shining white eyes and no hair, casts *his* eyes over the shadowed faces of the gathered fellowship, studying them, knowing they are ruthless in their endeavors. He himself looks tired, possibly ill. "We can't keep going back in time to kill time traveller's," he says. "In our reality they exist and if you take one out of the equation another one takes his place. We must deal with the spectrum of *time* instead. Take time out of the equation and everything changes. Everything we believe in! Everything we understand! So, if we stop the clock and end time, there will be no more rogue traveller's to circumvent the system. Isn't that a better solution to our problem?" His voice trembled.

"Well, it's one solution to our age-old problem!" says the Chairman. "But ending *time* would cause other problems."

"Indeed, nothing would be new and nothing would be old. No one would be born and no one would die. There would be no vices or virtues. No magic moments or diabolical problems and people *would* suffer more without *time* on their side, because it's the architect of our universe!" says the Vice-Chairman.

Shardlake shakes his head defiantly. "I still think the best solution to our problem is to go back in time and *kill* the son-of-a-bitch! Eradicate him once and for all!"

His words echo around the room and fade. Suddenly, the room becomes dark as the lights dim and there is a loud clanking sound and the smell of oil. Then something huge, made of metal, materialises, raising its visor, laying waste to the whole room, killing every single council member with its laser eyes chopping them to pieces, including Shardlake. Only a charred, blood-spattered room remains.

***

THE PRESENT DAY.
In my flat in London, the door opens. It's my wife Jane. I smile at her almost smugly. She still doesn't know of my time-travelling and never will. She'd think me mad.

She looks at me over the top of her glasses. "You're not looking very chipper this morning, darling," she says. "You look like you've been dragged through a hedge backwards and your clothes are a mess."

"I've been gardening!" I volunteer.

She stares at me oddly. "We haven't got a garden. We live in a flat and only have a window box!"

I stare back at her with a wider smile. We both laugh.

"That's pretty funny!" she says. "Why don't you go shower and clean up while I make us both something to eat and drink.

An hour later I've showered, shaved and we are eating lunch. I lean back in my chair and look at her. She's so beautiful. Tendrils of chestnut hair curl down, framing her face and her lips shimmer and her dark eyes glow with the vibrancy of life. She's shapely and tanned with long legs and slender ankles, looking amazingly fit for her age. But then, she is ten years younger than me.

I married the most wonderful woman in the world. And she's as beautiful now as when we first met.

"Do you feel any better now you've relaxed and eaten darling?" she asks.

I tell her "Yes," and we talk for a long while about various subjects. Everything from religion to the weather, art and artifacts, and time passes like a river of no return. But what my wife doesn't know is... that I could visit this conversation a million times over if I wanted to. And how strange is that? My significant other doesn't know that fact.

I smile. "Hey, why don't we go to the bedroom and fool around for a while? We haven't done that in ages. Or at least it seems ages!"

She laughs at my suggestion with a shudder of sheer delight. "And I thought the way to a man's heart was through his stomach."

"It is, but there are other ways too," I say.

"Okay, then why don't we go and explore those ways while I'm in the mood."

"Really?"

"Really, really!"

Five minutes later, my lips are firm against hers and I feel her warmth. She places her hand at the back of my neck, fingering my hair. Opening her lips she touches my tongue with hers and I go weak at the knees. My eyes are closed and I imagine what comes next. Her tongue tangles with mine and heat envelopes my brain. Her heat. She leans into me more and we fall onto the bed. "Make love to me,' she whispers in my ear.

I take her clothes off slowly, garment by garment, until she is naked, and then she does the same to me. Her legs lock about my hips, her nails raking my back as I enter her gently, lovingly, feeling more heat. "I've changed my mind. I want you to fuck me hard, and give me an orgasm like I've never had before," she whispers.

I kiss her lips gently, then repeatedly with increasing ardour, fondling and caressing her breasts as she moans and groans with short gasps of breathlessness. I begin to move with greater urgency for ten to fifteen minutes, increasing the rhythm and she sighs and moans, kissing my nipples and my lips. She scratches my back harder as she rises towards climax. More gasps of breathlessness. More moans. We climax together and I kiss her over and over, cuddling her into me. "You're beautiful," I say, "and I've loved you from the very first moment I saw you."

"Likewise," she admits, cuddling me even tighter.

My arm circles her waist and I hug her, kissing her full red lips softly. I'm a good lover, and she appreciates the tenderness of my skills usually. However, Jane's reaction to my advances were predictable today, because we haven't made love – HAD SEX – for quite some time, and I think she needed the release even more than I did.

"I'm a lucky man," I whisper.

"And I'm a lucky woman," Jane whispers back, and she relaxes her mind and we fall asleep in each other's arms and dream of even brighter days.

Chapter Eleven

It's the next morning and a thrilling quiver courses through my whole body as I recall last night. It was certainly a night for me to remember as I stare out of my living room window at a picture-perfect sunrise, painting a glowing skyline above London's tallest buildings. My eyes are filled with the glorious sight of a glimmering, golden day. *I am a lucky, lucky man,* I think to myself with a smile on my face.

My smile widens. I have an unbelievable power at my fingertips at any given moment, like a magic wand almost, to wave and do my bidding and even Mother Nature, as powerful as She is, cannot stop me from time-travelling. I have created a Masterpiece.

So where to now? What time-period should I visit? What riddle of the ages needs answering, and what is the single greatest unsolved mystery ever to baffle mankind? Well, I've visited with Jesus and know that God exists, at least in the minds of men, so I think the answer to that question is... are we *alone* in the universe? The next question then is, how can I solve this age old riddle? And one answer springs to mind! Did the Roswell Alien Incident of 1947 really happen? If it did, and the United States government have covered it up, the people of this planet need to know that we are *NOT* alone in the cosmos.

There have been many conspiracy theories surrounding this one event, with no solid conclusion to any of them, making the actual answer even more elusive and mystifying than it would be. Should I leap back to the town of Roswell and find out for myself, just because I can? And the answer to that question is a resounding yes!

I jump out of bed and dress quickly, shower, shave, brush my teeth and have a breakfast of bacon, eggs, toast and coffee.

I brush my teeth again. I'm ready to go. I search Wikipedia for details and coordinates, then set the Time Machine for the good old U.S.A in 1947, when an unknown object crashed on a ranch in the town of Roswell, New Mexico, on July 7th.

The local newspaper of the time, the Roswell Daily Record, announced on July 8th, in no uncertain terms, that the RAAF had captured a Flying Saucer in the region of Chaves County, and the explanation of what took place that day was based on official and unofficial communications. However, the most popular theory of what actually happened was that it was a craft of extraterrestrial origin that crash-landed with several ET's on board. This was categorically denied by the U.S.A.F., who maintained that the debris from the crash-site was nothing more than wreckage from a high altitude surveillance balloon that had come down and belonged to a top-secret project named Mogul.

But in stark contrast, many ufologists maintain that it was an alien craft that crashed, with its occupants captured for vivisection and study, which is why there *was* a cover-up. This then is the Holy Grail of all UFO sightings, because bodies of aliens were supposed to have been recovered intact, and then spirited away from the crash site to the infamous *AREA 51*. And the actual event is steeped in mystery, but tainted by skepticism, obviously.

Now I put my hand into my coat pocket, producing my machine with its parts of brass, nickel and ivory. I set the coordinates and press the 'GO' button once. I draw a breath. Grit my teeth. And the usual buzzing from the machine begins and grows louder and louder until the vibrating stops. I'm off at the speed of thought, travelling through the wormholes of *time* and complete darkness engulfs me.

***

I come to my senses, sometime later, in the middle of a desert road as a car almost runs me over. "Goddamn careless, good-for-nothing, son-of-a-bitch!" I roar. He drives around me, looking perplexed. There's a big old sun in front of me, high in the sky and it's scorching hot. I look around and seem to be a million miles from anywhere. And it is so, so hot. I would give anything to see a snowman right now, to steal his icicle nose and suck on it.

Well, I seem to have arrived in New Mexico and it's a vista of hot rock and desert sand with shimmering heat hazes, but somehow magnificently beautiful. I don't think I've ever seen so far on a clear day. But it is so, so hot! Oh, shut up and stop whining man... and get on with the task at hand, I chastise myself.

I notice the soles of my feet are burning. Red hot. In fact, I'll swear my shoes are on fire. Ouch! Luckily my brain is on auto-pilot and I begin to hop around like a bloody kangaroo for a few seconds, just to keep my feet *off* the ground. And as I'm hopping I notice a signpost further up the road, so I hop in that direction.

Finally I stand beneath the sign looking up and it reads: *AREA 51: GROOM LAKE IS A RESTRICTED AREA. KEEP OUT! DEADLY FORCE IS OPERATIONAL AND WILL BE USED AGAINST TRESPASSERS AND INTRUDERS.*

The warning sends a shiver down my spine like a sliver of ice. I turn away from the sign and stare around at the surrounding countryside, imagining a hand-picked sniper behind each rock and bush, taking aim at – *ME!* And that's frightening. *My face must be grim right now,* I think to myself.

I shrink back away from the sign, wheel around a couple of times searching the vista of rock and sand, my eyes narrowing, looking for signs of life. I see nothing. No living soul or crawling creature. A deafening silence prevails, except for the almost inaudible hum from the twenty foot high electrified fence that stretches for as far as the eye can see in every direction.

In my mind, a sharp frightening hiss rips through the still air. I think of the 70s TV program, The Twilight Zone. Another shiver runs down my spine. *I could be abducted at any moment by covert C.I.A operatives and spirited away, never to be seen or heard from again,* I think to myself, when suddenly the sky is filled with helicopters from out of the south-west, buzzing around me with men shouting through megaphones, not to move. Guns of various shapes and sizes are aiming at me. I'm peppered with red dots from laser sights. My mind snaps back to reality and the daydream is gone. "Damn that's scary!" I mutter to myself. But it *could* happen.

"Well, then, here you are wandering around in the desert!" announces a voice from behind, startling me.

I turn around quickly. The speaker, standing about ten feet away, is a bizarre caricature of some 1960s flower-power pop singer. He's tall and thin, well over six feet, but so lean as to be almost stick-like and he's on the other side of the electrified fence, smiling at me.

"Who are you?" I ask.

"You can get shot for being out here," says the stranger.

I stare at him. "I'd say you're the one who will get shot for being on that side of the fence!"

He stares back at me twice as hard. "Wrong! You're the one who's standing on restricted ground in a U.S.A.F. air base, and the guy who nearly ran you over is almost certainly a soldier who's gone for help!"

My thinking falters. There is silence for a moment.

"I'm out here writing a book about *strange phenomenon* and you appear on that side of the fence from out of thin air!" he says, looking at me as if I'm an ghost.

Now I consider where I'm standing. There are and will always be risks in life, but it's meant to be lived that way, because if it isn't, what is the purpose of living? Calculating those risks are what's necessary, but experiencing them is essential!

"Well, that entirely depends on how well I can handle myself, if caught, doesn't it?" I counter, pressing the *SPECTRAL* button on my machine. I vanish right before his eyes, leaving him scratching his head in dismay. He hesitates, then hurries on his way as if he *has* seen a ghost! And except for that one guy, the whole landscape seems lifeless. In fact, it looks so desolate that I could be on the Goddamn moon. But it's so, so hot and I realise I'm thirsty.

I walk for a couple of miles, heading in a North-easterly direction, following the state highway by the side of the fence, just to see where it leads. When I feel safe I click *SPECTRAL* off for a while and a nearby jackrabbit that spots me is startled and hurries noiselessly for cover. Following it, I discover a pool of water in a sheltered clearing. Taking off my hat I wipe the sweat-band with my forefinger, snapping the moisture off. I fling myself down and drink from the surface of the pool with short gulps, snorting into the water like a hog.

Don't drink so much, I tell myself. *I'll get sick if it's tainted.*
Finally I dip my head under the water a couple of times and sit back up on the bank with the water running down my shirt, front and back, but it's so, so refreshing. I stare at my reflection in the pool and the rims of my eyes are red with the sun's glare. They feel sore too. I put my hat back on, lowering the brim to keep the sun out of my eyes and lay back on the sand with my hands crossed behind my head. Then for some considerable time I lay listening.

It's now mid-day, the sun is high overhead and an hour passes slowly as I relax. Then suddenly I hear voices. Two at least. Both men. I jerk upwards, looking around, but see no one. I click my machine to *SPECTRAL* again.

"Reese, we've been out here an hour now and seen no one,"

comes a gruff voice.

"Listen, he's out here on this base somewhere, 'cause I almost ran the guy over," replies a second voice.

"Well, whatta we do now?"

"We keep lookin', that's what! Otherwise we'll be the ones in chains when we get back to base!"

"Yeah, I suppose we'd better find the crazy son-of-a-bitch or we'll be in hot water when we get back." There is the loud click of rifles loading as the voices slowly recede into the distance. I lay back down with my hands behind my head again and fall asleep for a few hours.

***

It's dark by the time I wake and there's a light comforting breeze, but it's getting colder by the minute. Standing I stretch, dusting myself down and then I climb to the top of a rise. In the distance I can see lights from a vast complex that's brightly lit by the tallest watchtowers and rectangular building that looks like a giant airplane hangar, similar in size to the one that houses the space shuttle.

That's it! I tell myself. *The heart of AREA 51!* And of course, there are guards patrolling everywhere in two's and four's. *Wonder what's really in that hanger? Aliens? Alien craft? Alien artifacts? Well, I'm here now in Spectral form and I damn-well intend to find out!*

I walk on in the darkness, clearing the rise, and start my decent towards the complex, watching the searchlights shining all over the place. They hit me time and again, but pass straight through my formless body like a torchlight through glass. A heat-haze is more visible than I am right now.

For a moment I stop and think. *What I discover in that huge hanger may change my life forever! Am I ready for that? And the answer is: I think I'll only know if and when I discover alien life-*

forms. Can that be anymore mind-blowing than discovering Time Travel?

I pick up the pace and begin to run. Well, I've always enjoyed exercise and it kick-starts the metabolism after a sleep. Now I'm less than two hundred yards from the complex and the biggest building I've ever seen in my life. Big enough to house several space shuttles, including the booster rockets and gantry. Warily I approach, the searchlight beams penetrating the fabric of my body. Guards are milling around everywhere, going about their sentry duty, unaware of my presence, thankfully.

Finally I'm standing by a locked door when a uniformed officer appears. He keys in a ten digit number, waits for about three seconds, then has his retina scanned by a small telescopic screen that pushes its way out of a round hole in the side of the doorway. "Identity verified and accepted," says the com-link from inside the facility.

The lock tumblers in the middle of the door begin to spin. Cryptic symbols and numbers that I've never seen before revolve, until one by one they click into the right combination. And as the last tumbler clanks into place, there is a sound indicating that the locks are being withdrawn. Gears spin and it opens, reminding me of a bank-vault door. It's about ten feet tall and almost as thick, made of layer upon layer of a special alloy, much, much tougher than any steel I suspect. I walk in behind the officer. We pace about fifty yards to a similar door where the whole process is repeated, but instead of the ten digit code and retina scan, the com-link asks for a password, to which the officer replies *'PROJECT AURORA'*. The door inches open slowly in the same manner as the previous one.

My God, getting into Fort Knox would be easier, I think to myself as we enter together, and inside it's a labyrinth of wide alleys built on several levels with steel and Perspex lifts of varying sizes and shapes passing each other silently. Armed guards are patrolling everywhere. I smile to myself jubilantly. No one. And I mean *NO ONE* without top security clearance from the highest level of government could *EVER* get in here! But I have, with the aid of my machine.

Jeez, does that make me a spy. I feel like a real life Ethan Hunt from the Mission Impossible films. I picture myself coming down from the roof on a rope or wire, avoiding the infra-red censors, while bypassing hi-tech alarm systems. *God, that would be child's play compared to what I've just done!*

The officer marches purposefully over to a huge machine with four monstrously big wheels and climbs up into the cab, beckoning for a guard to climb up the ladder into the passenger seat, which he does. Obviously I have no idea what the machine is or what it's capable of doing, so I climb up onto the back of it as it takes off down the widest of all alleyways, a circular tunnel of extraordinary size that seems to be heading for the bowels of the earth, literally, and has been gouged out of the solid rock under the facility by another huge machine. Probably something similar in size to the boring machine used to dig the Channel Tunnel. But the walls are like black glass and are so smooth that they look like they've been cut by a laser.

Minute after minute we travel at approximately twenty miles per hour for what seems an eternity, until we come to an underground lake. A veritable *sea* of green. It stretches for as far as I can see and is lit by artificial light that is so strong it makes me squint, until I become accustomed to it. The vehicle comes to a shuddering halt, tyres squealing. The officer opens the cab door and climbs out, sliding down the ladder with ease. The guard does the same and they head towards a dizzying array of more massive machines that I've never seen anywhere before, which I marvel at. They remind me of the

Thunderbirds, from the TV series of the same name, but they're bigger, dull in colour and have no visible welded seams or rivets. And even the adjective *gigantic* doesn't describe their immense size.

A thought now occurs to me. *Is the land above called Groom Lake because there was a lake there too and it's somehow ended up down here?* It's certainly a possibility. Stranger things have happened, particularly to me! I stare at the machines. They vary in size and shape, have clearly seen better days and are showing their age. Also they smell funny, reeking of what I can only describe as a mixture of oil, tar and something like sulphur. It's a strange smell.

I look up at the curved rocky ceiling that would be a sky if we weren't underground and wonder how these machines arrived here on this sandy shore. Then, as if in answer to my wondering, the surface of the lake erupts into great waves, foaming and bubbling as another colossal, strange looking machine walks out of the water, onto the shore, clanking along with perfect, unfaltering movements, blowing steam in ragged geysers from its underbelly as it goes. The noise is deafening. *This is getting stranger by the second. It's like something out of a Jules Verne novel,* I think to myself as the newcomer grinds to a halt in front of us.

At that, a black canopy opens at the top of the machine in a final puff of steam and something rises from a seat in the cockpit and exits. A tall black shape. An oddity that would stand out in a crowd and be the object of stares. And definitely *NOT* human!

Chapter Twelve

Shrill sounds that are almost musical come from the demonic looking helmet of the newcomer. I take in the sight and shiver. My blood curdles. *Either the thing is made of metal and bone or it's wearing a seriously ominous looking exoskeleton.*

The officer's face is deadly serious. The guard's too. My mouth is hanging open as I stare wide eyed at whatever is climbing down the long metal ladder towards us in an ungainly fashion, still making what seems to be shrill music.

Halfway down the ladder it stops suddenly, surveying the landscape below, then carries on climbing down until it finally reaches the bottom. Turning to face the three of us it looks awesomely powerful, but I can't tell if it's a creature of some kind or a robot. Disconnecting its life-line to the mother-ship, the shrill sound stops and its visor lifts slowly. A green glow pulsates. There is a palpable silence for a moment.

"The ARK is *full* and ready to sail," it finally announces in a deep, resonant voice, "and a considerable cross-section of humankind and animals will be saved!"

I stare at the thing. It stares back. *Can it see me somehow, even though I'm in Spectral form?* I wonder. *No, it's impossible, I'm invisible to the naked eye. Unless it has a different type of vision like infra-red or heat-vision? Anyway, what's this about an Ark?*

The officer is about to speak, but stops as he, the guard and I back away slightly from out of the shadow of the thing. It's very intimidating to say the least, even though it seems friendly, but I swear it *is* looking straight at me. My pulse shoots into the red zone and I'm quite freaked out, but I hold my ground hoping I'm wrong and things won't get ugly for me.

Suddenly the officer's radio comes to life, ordering him to escort the newcomer to AREA 47 for debriefing, so they casually usher the *thing* into the transporter we arrived in and shoot off down the tunnel, back in the direction from which we'd come, leaving me wondering about AREA 47. I stare at the strange craft that towers over me and then look around. I'm completely alone.

I decide to investigate the Walker. *Well, in for a penny, in for a pound, I always say!*

I begin to climb the ladder, leading up to the cockpit, counting each rung as I go and, *Oh my God*, what a climb it is. Three hundred steps later, I have quite a view from the cockpit which looks alien to me. I've been in trains, planes and automobiles, seen and studied their mechanical workings, but never have I seen anything like this. It looks almost organic inside, like the spacecraft in the hit motion picture, *Alien*. There are no hinges on the doors, no seams in the walls and no rivets or bolts to be seen anywhere, as if the craft was produced in *one* giant piece. But surely, that's not possible.

I sit in the seat where the controls should be, but there aren't any. *Are these giant machines new weapons of mass destruction, secreted away, here in the New Mexico desert, ready and waiting for World War 3 to happen? Or are they different types of alien spacecraft, covertly spirited away from various crash-sites, brought here to AREA 51 to be hidden from the world? For they all seem to be huddled together, standing guard over this underground beach, maybe patrolling somewhere every once in a while, looking for any impending danger that might raise its ugly head – while I simply mark the passage of time.*

Suddenly, there's a bone-shaking jolt and the cockpit door closes, locking me inside. I'm panic-stricken as otherworldly voices enter my head and protoplasmic screens open up before my eyes, showing me images I don't understand and cannot make sense of. I collapse back into the chair which seems to hug me tightly, taking my breath away.

What the hell is happening? What evil doings or dark forces are at work here? I breathe hard, panicking, struggling for air and groan as the seat hugs me harder. Then a voice in my head says: *you weren't safe out there, but are in here – are you ready for the ride of your life?*

I theorize, or rather I daydream, that I'm in some experimental high speed jet, yet to be tested, with a capability of 6 times the speed of sound, carrying a payload of bombs even more destructive than the atom or hydrogen bombs and no one in the outside world, other than high ranking officials know what the hell is going on here at AREA 51.

There's another bone-jarring jolt and the craft groans as some sort of power-source comes online. The Walker turns in a semi-circle like a giant soldier coming to attention, then heads out into the lake, going deeper and deeper until the cockpit submerges beneath the waves in a final flurry of air bubbles. I can't see a thing for a few moments, except for a glowing sheen of blue on the cockpit window on the inside and tiny bubbles rising toward the surface on the outside.

The Walker and I descend into the darkness, then huge spotlights blink on illuminating the gloomy depths as the machine's powerful legs propel me through the water effortlessly. However, the machine falters momentarily when navigating a wide crack in the lake bed and I pitch forward, banging my head with a yelp.

Don't be afraid, the voice in my head murmurs, *we belong together, you and I, and I will take care of you.*

Relaxing a little because of the soothing, reassuring words, I'm still overwhelmed by what's happening to me. "Where are you taking me?" I ask nervously.

I'm taking you to see the ARK. Well, seeing is believing isn't it?

There is no way of doubting it, the Walker isn't a machine. It's something else. An entity of some kind that can read my thoughts. Now every nerve ending in my body feels like a live wire. "Are you from another world?" I ask. To this question there is no reply.

You must choose between the life you know and an unknown destiny that beckons you forever! The voice replies. *For your destiny is a thrill-a-minute, fast, fun-filled adventure in the making!*

I'm beginning to feel like Captain Nemo, from the underwater adventure film 20,000 Leagues Under The Sea, when suddenly there is a violent jolt and I grunt as one of the Walker's giant feet hit and squash what appears to be a large crustacean. However, the Walker travels on relentlessly, and through the darkness of the murky water in the narrow beam of the search light, something gigantic and shiny comes into view in the distance.

I squint, rubbing the condensation from the window on the cockpit door, trying to get a better look at what's up ahead, when all manner of coloured lights flicker on and illuminate the biggest machine I have seen in my entire life. A craft of impossibly colossal proportions, shaped like a squid, but so large, in fact, that twenty aircraft carriers would probably fit inside.

My ride is expertly handled by the Walker doing its job as my escort through the debris-filled lake, with countless wrecked machines littering the lake bed, and it looks like a scene from World War 2. Also, I can see images from inside the Ark on the protoplasmic screen above my head. I gape at the monitor which isn't really there. It's just a collection of protoplasmic photons in reality, but it looks real enough to touch. I focus on an image of oddly shaped pens, thousands of them, with two animals in each, and I can only assume that one is male and the other female, seeing as how the Walker called this mighty craft an Ark. Most are familiar. Some are not, and are the strangest looking animals I have ever seen. The images change constantly from one pen to another, and a sort of monitor at the bottom of the screen is obviously checking temperatures inside the pens to keep the animals comfortable and in a stable environment.

Staring at the pictures, I wonder what animals will appear next. A gorilla's face suddenly fills the screen, grunting, and scares the life out of me. Nervously I laugh with relief when it disappears again. Then I hear a low rumble, the lights dim and a huge metal door in the side of the craft opens like a giant star-shaped camera lens as we approach. Wider and wider it opens, until the largest whale could swim through it. I stare in wonder. *How on earth does anyone build something this big?* And even my imagination isn't capable of answering that question.

The Walker and I enter the cavernous hole and it closes slowly behind us as we rise towards the surface inside the Ark – a surreal moment if ever there was one. *Will the bubble burst when I wake up, because I MUST be asleep and dreaming, Nothing of this world can be so... big!* I think to myself.

"Is the Ark nuclear? How did it get here? And what country made it... the USA? " I ask.

Questions! Questions! All will be answered in due course, announces the Walker.

We hit the surface and the Walker is plucked from the water by a huge crane with a claw that plants us safely on dry land. Reveling in the experience, I am in awe of what is happening around me, because never have I seen such a sight. It's beyond all imagination.

The Walker whirls in an arc, flanked by two other monstrously big machines that seem to exchange glances and nod. We walk together, the machines and I, to where an army of machines await, and they are other-worldly looking like the Walker, having no seams, bolts or rivets. Dust kicked up by the machines movements blur my vision momentarily, but then I see them all salute us as we pass. Finally my Walker sits on what appears to be a throne of gold and the cockpit door opens with a puff of steam. Climbing out, I am saluted by the other machines as if I'm some sort of visiting dignitary.

"Commander in Chief, we have awaited your coming for a very long time!" announces one of the machines.

I look at the machines, from one to another, and await the Walker's response, but it says nothing. Not one word. Climbing down the long ladder I look around me, and on reaching the red concrete floor I stare upward at the wall of towering Walkers. They are as mountainous summits with puffs of steam that swirl and stir about their cockpits like mist on a cold morning, yet it's as if they are breathing and exhaling slowly. I peer about warily, when suddenly a voice booms from behind me.

"Well, then, here you are at last, back where you belong, Time Traveller!"

Swinging around, I come face to face with my older, wiser looking future-self. But how can that be? And to be honest, the answer is simple. My present-self has the ability to, by way of the Time Machine, visit any time-period, past, present or future, so the Laws of Physics make it possible for me to exist in two places at the same time. I stare at my other-self. He's ninety years old if he's a day. White hair. White goatee beard and moustache, but God, he... I... we still look good for our age.

My future-self is dressed in blue robes, adorned by an array of beautifully coloured sashes and he looks more like a mystic or a soothsayer than a professor. A large crystal hangs about his neck and he's guided by a walking stick as he steps closer to me, smiling with the broadest of grins. "Welcome, my boy, you're just in time for tea and an explanation of how and why Area 51 and this undersea facility exists because, by the astonished look on your face, I can see you thought it didn't exist. However, Area 51 is where you created and constructed these colossal automaton's – semi-mechanical contrivances, constructed to act independently as if by their own power."

"*I* created all this? When did I do this impossible feat?" I ask in disbelief.

"No! *We* created all this!" says my future-self with a smile of satisfaction.

"I had no idea. And I'm no longer certain what brought me here to this place. I'm only certain of one thing now, that it's hard to accept what you're telling me – that I... We designed and built all of this!"

"Destiny brought you here, my boy. We are Time Traveller's and know what the future holds for planet earth. We have built this Ark in readiness for a cataclysmic event that will happen in the near future."

"But I've seen the end of the world and it's a billion years hence," I respond.

"We are preparing for a cataclysmic event, not the end of the world. A flood of biblical proportions, caused by the sinking of an island in the South Pacific ocean, after a volcanic eruption, will create a tsunami that will devastate many lands. A wall of water, one thousand feet high, will circle the globe, drowning many," says my future-self, ominously. "We have detected a gas pocket beneath the island and it will blow very soon!"

I am staggered by the news of this coming event. "What are we to do?"

"The only thing we can do, my boy! Save as many lives as possible in the coming week. We have an estimated seven days before our time runs out. *Luckily*, the Ark is ready and outfitted with every possible essential to sustain life for a whole year, it being the size of a small island. Hydroponics on board are capable of growing enough food to sustain an army, and a very large army at that! We also have a meat production plant, which leaves the meat a bit *stringy*, but tasty if nothing else. And for vegetarians there is a quorn assembly plant in operation. We even have a sizable library on board for those who want to digest words." My future self, chuckles to himself at the thought.

Suddenly my attention is diverted away from him to what looks like a vending machine in a corner of the room, filled with chocolate bars and fruity drinks. To my utter surprise and amazement it sprouts three legs, walks towards us and a compartment at the top begins boiling and serving coffee to several officers who appear from a backroom and wait patiently in line to be served, while absentmindedly watching a video link on its side.

I swing my head back around, fixing my future-self's gaze. "I suppose *we* invented that walking vending machine too?"

"No, silly, that was a vending machine company called Vend-all! We only invent life-changing things, my boy," he replies with a wry smile.

Finally the officers are served and return to the room from whence they came, along with the buzz of their conversation. The vending machine returns to the corner of the room, retracts its legs and settles back down with a hiss of steam puffing from the coffee compartment. Two coin slots close like a pair of eyes and it makes a gentle snoring sound as if it's falling asleep.

"Wow, weird! Who thinks up a machine like that? They must have some imagination," say I.

My future self, laughs with a huff. "Oh, not something that we could dream up then?"

I laugh too, seeing the irony, having invented several of the strangest machines ever, including a Time Machine small enough to place into your pocket.

I walk to the base of a staircase and look down into a huge hangar where a single vehicle sits alone, hovering just above the ground, but it's like no other I've ever seen – disc shaped with lights of many colours circling its outer perimeter in a slow controlled fashion. I descend the staircase until I'm stood in its shadow. Its lights glow like a kaleidoscope and seem to form a rainbow over the strange craft. There's an open hatch and a set of steps leading up into it. Cautiously I approach, mindful of any danger that might lurk inside. Climbing slowly, warily, craning my neck around the doorway, I enter.

It's pitch black inside. I feel my way around until my hand catches on something. Bright lights blink several times and then come on and remain on. They dazzle me and I cover my eyes until I'm used to the glare. Lowering my hands, I'm astonished by what I see.

Chapter Thirteen

The outside of the craft appears to be about forty metres in diameter, but the inside seems fifty time that size and isn't an optical illusion. Suddenly the hatch closes behind me with a soft hiss and a puff of steam. I'm trapped. Now I'm committed to search for a way out at some point.

Inside the colossal room where I'm standing, there's the buzz of machinery. However, it's an unfamiliar room with an unfamiliar echoing resonance that fills my mind with endless pictures of ancient earthly monuments, vital statistics, mathematical formula, longitude and latitude in relation to a Prime Meridian line – but it's not from Greenwich in England. It's from Egypt and the line passes through the Giza Pyramid. I see the great structure, made of over 2 million stone blocks. It's got four 90 degree sides, each with a 51 degree slope, a volume of more than 91 million cubic feet with an estimated area of 559,320 sq feet and its original height *was* 480 feet when it was built 4700 years ago.

Stonehenge replaces the vision and I see it before it fell into ruin. It has 30 lintels in a perfect 360 degree arc, held aloft by 30 supporting stones and a horseshoe shape in the middle with 5 lintels held aloft by 10 stones. An equation replaces the vision. 60 x 360 (that's the 60 stones x the 360 degree arc of the circle) = 21,000, which conveys a hidden number of 51 degrees, divided by 10 minutes, divided 42.35 seconds of latitude – the exact position of Stonehenge on our modern maps. Impossible, but true.

The visions speed up and I see the sunken city of Yonaguni, Japan. Shen-hsi, China. Cuzco, Peru. Easter Island in the Pacific. Machu Pichu, Peru. And an endless array of archeological sites before they fell into ruin. Another mass of equations invade my mind too, making me dizzy. I scream,

"STOP! STOP!" It doesn't stop, but does slow right down, showing me the earth from space with a straight line at a 30 degree angle to the equator, and it runs through each and every one of the ancient sites and cities.

Suddenly the vision changes back to the Giza pyramid. An imaginary arc is drawn inside the base of the pyramid. A second arc is drawn outside. The length of the inside circle subtracted from the length of the outside circle = 299,337,984. It's the speed of light at millions of metres per second.

What are the machines in this room showing me? I suddenly remember an article I once read: "In 1859, John Taylor discovered that if you divide one dimension of the pyramid by another, it equals PI – the mathematical formula." *Could it be that the ancients had worked out global positioning? But how? It can only be done from space with the aid of satellites. However, every ancient monument I am shown explains exactly where it is on earth by multiplying or dividing its structure in a particular way. And that is pure genius!*

I'm astounded, yet not surprised, by what I am being shown. I have long suspected that there were ancient civilizations, thousands or even millions of years ago, far more advanced than we are today. Strange artifacts like copper nails, amber buttons and even skulls with bullet holes in them have been discovered inside seams of coal millions of years old. There's no way on earth of faking that. It's impossible if you know anything about how coal forms.

Snapping back from my reverie I turn, feeling eyes burning into me.

"Greetings Earthling!" a voice intones kindly from behind.

I turn, fixing the creature with a baleful stare, but a harmless one. "What are you? And where did you come from?"

The creature is silent and hesitates before answering. "The

truth is, I am what you call... an *alien*, and I came from the future... just like you."

I'm standing silently, taking in the enormity of my situation. *History in the making! This is it! I knew there was intelligent life out in the universe,* my mind murmurs. Then the creature produces a ray gun from a hidden pocket in its silver space suit and aims it at my face. Shit! I never expected that! I stare at the gun, a futuristic looking weapon if ever I've seen one. Panic floods through me. I look up, horrified. I'm going to die! The alien pulls the trigger, staring at me as a giant might at a bothersome fly. I freeze, fearing the worst, hoping I'll feel no pain, praying for a quick death. I'm squirted on the forehead and the alien laughs with great gusto. My future-self pulls off a rubber mask as the water drips down my reddened face.

"Sorry, my boy, couldn't resist it! Just a little light-hearted humour!" he announces.

I shake my head, not knowing whether to laugh or cry, I'm so relieved. "Damn that was exciting, but terrifying!"

"Walk with me a while, my boy, and let's converse, for there is much to say."

I shrug. "Okay."

"The Ark has been a work in progress," says my future-self, "but now it's finished and it's an extraordinary craft, conceived and constructed by the two of us, by back-engineering the small alien craft that crash landed at Roswell in New Mexico..."

We walk, chattering on about the Ark, aliens, alien technology and all related subjects, including Darwin's *Theory of Evolution* as we wander through the vast room.

"...These are huge issues," he continues. "According to the fossil records, conventional evolution does not account for the Cambrian Explosion, 500 million years ago, when almost all major animal groups first appeared, and the reason for that is – extraterrestrials put them here as a genetic experiment. That's why virtually all major animal groups made their first appearance in this geologic period, and it refutes Darwin's conventional view of evolution through natural selection.

"In fact, fossil records prove that the direct ancestors of man also existed at the time of the Cambrian Explosion, and that their evolution must have happened impossibly quickly for Darwin's theory to be correct. Needless to say, it isn't correct as it doesn't account for the new genetic forms that appeared all at once, and the people of the world need to know these facts."

My future-self talks incessantly and I listen intently, until he comes around to the events of the present day.

"...Shadow governments are springing up all over, elected by no one and accountable to no one, and aliens are involved and as real as you or I, my boy. This morning the Canadian Minister for Defense finally admitted to the media that at least four different species of extraterrestrials have been visiting the earth for millions of years, and each has a different agenda.

"Unseen aliens walk amongst us at the present time and one species, the Tall Whites, are working with the American government even as we speak, sharing their technology. The cosmos, as we always suspected, is teaming with intelligent life that is far more advanced than we are, but the scary part is that some species of aliens have a malevolent agenda towards us, and they are the ones responsible for the abductions, experimentation and murder. At the core of their plan they want to take over our world and enslave us all!"

I shake my head in disbelief after listening to this. I'm lost for words – a silent audience. Our long walk finally brings us to a glass display case that is about four foot square, and on show are two footprints embedded in a rock sample that is over 100 million years old, found in Montana, USA. A booted foot has left a print inside a huge dinosaur's footprint. But how can this be? According to archeologists, man was not around at the time of the dinosaurs and did not invent footwear until as late as 10,000 years ago.

I take several moments to collect my thoughts, focusing on the display. Now I picture the world through a Time Traveller's eyes and it's completely different from what I was taught at school. The teachers had built the foundation of my understanding one block at a time, but some were obviously in the wrong order and some even false. You see, not everything we learn in life is as it seems when we learn it. Even the statement, "*I think, therefore I am,*" is a contradiction if we study it long enough. History should teach us, *not* our fellow man. We should search for possible solutions to our conundrums, but make no attempt to subvert the course of history in doing so. At least that's my opinion. Well, actually, it's *our* opinion, seeing as how we two Time traveller's are one and the same person.

Suddenly the Ark is jolted, rolling from side to side. "What the hell?" I say as I'm knocked from my feet. My future-self falls by my side, striking his head on a bulkhead door, knocking him unconscious. There's another jolt, even more violent than the first, accompanied by a loud rumbling sound that echoes eerily throughout the whole vessel. Nearby lights sparkle with overloaded energy and bulbs explode, showering me with glass and sparks that light the air. This causes great concern as I have no idea what's happening around me.

I stare up at the localised viewing screens, scattered around the room, which show various images of the inside and outside of the Ark, but see no danger. I stand up quickly, running to the nearest sensory equipment. It shows strange vibrations on a graph, getting stronger and stronger by the second, with an energy powerful enough to shake the bedrock of the sea beneath us, causing massive waves to form, rocking the Ark from side to side.

I'm certain it's an undersea earthquake, like my future-self predicted. I run back to him, but am so stunned by what's happening around me that I'm making inarticulate sounds instead of coherent words, indicating my level of stress. Finally, I manage to rouse him from his unconscious stupor and I tell him what's happening, then help him to the bridge of the Ark where he slumps to a chair gasping for breath.

"I do believe the apocalypse is upon us," he murmurs, staring at the screen in front of him. It shows a volcano erupting and an island blowing itself to pieces, causing huge waves one thousand feet tall to form in the surrounding sea. The scene is like hell on earth and a coldness seems to settle in our bones as we watch the island blow apart and sink beneath the sea, causing even greater waves to form. We huddle together, watching in disbelief as a million tons of rock vanishes in an instant with both of use thinking the same thing, that the eruption of Krakatoa, east of Java, in 1883 must have seemed like a damp squib compared to this cataclysm.

Luckily, the indigenous inhabitants of the island were evacuated some days earlier and brought aboard the Ark, so there are no casualties – however, the huge waves will certainly circle the globe, killing millions of people, and nothing can protect them from a watery grave.

Suddenly, I hear a door opening behind us. "Professor, the Ark is sinking! It's sinking!" comes a voice. I turn and see a panicked officer wearing a life jacket.

"That's not possible," says my future-self, looking traumatised.

"The Ark is holed and we're facing shipwreck! We hit

something that rose up from the rocky bottom and even though this ship is a radical size and fitted with watertight bulkheads and doors, nothing can stop us from sinking!"

I race to the holed area and am staggered by the size of the breech. The cargo-hold is flooding fast and nothing can be done to stop the water pouring through. The Ark is doomed and destined to sink. Then I have an instant brainstorm. *Wait a minute! The Time Machine has special features and functions, hardly tested I know, but anything is worth a try!* I jerk the machine from my pocket, turning it on, and the crystal face glows. Scrolling to the third screen I hesitate, hovering my fingertips over the four tiny dials at its centre, feeling my heart racing as I press the first one.

Suddenly, a familiar voice announces, "Super-Electromagnet on, Time Traveller!" The lights dim, there's a breath of wind and then an almighty clatter as everything metallic – cars, cabinets, tables and chairs and the like – catapults across the ship's cargo hold like bullets from a gun, filling the breech. I press the second dial.

"Which gas do you require to be, Time Traveller?"

"Oxyacetylene!" I shout, lighting up like a blow torch, welding the metal together, sealing the hole. I return to my normal state. Pressing the third dial, my bodily matter is transferred into energy and I dispel the thousands of tons of water, evaporating it in seconds. I tell the machine to cancel my order and as its cogs and gears whirr, my molecules rearrange themselves and I return to my former state again. Now everything around me looks normal.

I race back to the control room, where my future-self is trying to bring the Ark back under control and on course. He's breathless and struggling to right the vessel when there's another a deep sustained rumble, louder this time, that echoes eerily throughout every corridor. *Have we been holed again, or run aground? What the hell is happening?*

My future-self looks horrified, staring at the battery of gauges and dials in front of him. "The atomic reactor is in *Melt-Down*, according to the readouts!"

"Can we trust the readouts?" I ask, hoping to hear the word 'NO'!

"Mother of God!" my future-self breathes softly, terror in his tone, fear shining in his eyes. "We're all going to die!"

Suddenly an urgent female voice interrupts my reverie of terrified thoughts. "Ben, get here right now!"

My mind reels in a kind of fog, trying process everything that's happening around me.

I stare at the gauges and dials, watching them rise into the Red Zone, approaching critical mass. *We are going to die!*

"Ben, times up!" comes the female voice again, but I'm befogged of mind and can't quite get a grasp of who it is. I'm busy wondering how I can save the Ark and the thousands of lives on board. I say nothing, concentrating harder on the diabolical problem at hand.

Finally my mother bursts into my bedroom, looking furious. "Your tea's ready and on the table going cold! You can daydream about being a *Time Traveller* all you like later, now get down stairs this instant!" She stomps back down into the dining room, arms folded across her chest.

"But everyone on the Ark is about to *die* and I've only a few more pages to read!" I reply, staring at myself in the dressing table mirror, a glint of defiance in my eyes.

I stare harder at my reflection. Suddenly, it becomes hazy and the house lights flicker momentarily. Then my reflection vanishes completely and I pass out.

***

I come back to my senses, sometime later, listening to the steady tick of the Grandfather clock outside my bedroom door. *I must have fallen asleep while reading. I wish I was a Time Traveller like the one in my books. But then, I am just seven years old and a compulsive daydreamer. Great read though, my comic books, like journals of something that has really happened. Oh, well, better go downstairs for tea before my mom gets really angry and takes my Time Travel comics away, to burn them like she threatened to do yesterday.* I'll hide them under my big old wardrobe. She'll never look there. She never does!

Then, I seem to hear another voice echoing around me. Startled I glance around, but there's no one there.

"Not a wise thing to do, visiting ones younger-self. It drains your strength, Time Traveller, but you just had to come back here and see where it all began, didn't you? You just had to! To remember where your destiny was first realised, and you'll probably do it, *time* and *time* again!" says the metallic sounding voice. A new image flickers momentarily in my dressing table mirror. An old man with white hair, a goatee beard and a moustache is smiling back at me. A giant robot with laser-like eyes is standing by his side. But they disappear, replaced by my own reflection.

Did I really see my future-self and Nav-Man? Or am I just tired and my imagination is running wild again? Well, I really wouldn't want it any other way, would you?

...TO BE CONTINUED...

__Time is the Architect of our Universe.__

<u>Did intelligence preceed speech?</u>
<u>Or did speech nurture our intelligence?</u>

About the Author.

Michael Siddall was born in Sheffield, South Yorkshire, England, and his aspirations to become a novelist began after devising the board game: 'A Challenge of the Gods'. Educated at Newfield School in Sheffield he left with exemplary grades in his final exams and went on to Granville College for two years, where he studied art and design, literature and history. Times were hard and he left college to become a carpet fitter.

As a child of nine Michael contracted Rheumatic Fever, spending a whole year in the Northern General Hospital laid flat on his back for the first six months and in a wheelchair for the following six. To occupy himself he wrote his first short stories and poems. He has continued to write every day of his life since.

He was told that as a consequence of his illness he would have a weak heart and spend the rest of his life in a wheelchair. Michael proved the specialists wrong. Not only did he walk again; he joined the army and became a P.T. I. in the R.E.M.E., stationed at Borden in Hampshire. He has also attained 5th Dan Black Belts with Instructor status in Shotokan Karate, Aikido, Korean Kempo and teaches his friends Kick-boxing and Mixed Martial Arts in his spare time.

A writer since school, he has written several Works of varying length, 'The Blackhawks Impossible Quest' being his first serious attempt at fantasy novel writing after taking a creative writing course. He has also written the three part novel, 'A Violent Man', the time travel novels, 'All the Time in the World' and 'Time and Time again', besides 'The Book, the Wand, the Magic'. He still resides in Sheffield where he ice skates almost every day at Ice Sheffield, particularly on Saturday and Sunday mornings, amongst an array of treasured friends and colleagues.

MICHAEL SIDDALL Sponsors TINT STUDIO:
Window Film Specialists.

AUTOMOTIVE, COMMERCIAL, RESIDENTIAL, CONSEVATORIES, SAFETY FILMS.

WWW.tintstudio.co.uk

Unit 1, Sheaf Gardens Industrial Estate, Sheffield, South Yorkshire, England.

Telephone: 0114 2759922

555

Printed in Dunstable, United Kingdom